# Hummingbird

# Hummingbird

Kimberly Greene Angle

Farrar Straus Giroux
New York

www.fsgkidsbooks.com

Library of Congress Cataloging-in-Publication Data
Angle, Kimberly Greene.
    Hummingbird / Kimberly Greene Angle.— 1st ed.
        p.   cm.
    Summary: In spite of a busy life on the family pumpkin and watermelon
farm in Jubilee, Georgia, twelve-year-old March Anne Tanner feels that
something is missing, and when Grenna, the grandmother who has helped
raise her since her mother died when she was three, also passes on, March
Anne finds that she must act on her feelings of loss.
    ISBN-13: 978-0-374-33376-8
    ISBN-10: 0-374-33376-9
    [1. Farm life—Georgia—Fiction.   2. Family life—Georgia—Fiction.
3. Grandmothers—Fiction.   4. Loss (Psychology)—Fiction.   5. Grief—Fiction.
6. Death—Fiction.   7. Georgia—Fiction.]   I. Title.

PZ7.A5838Hu 2008
[Fic]—dc22
                                                              2007009156

For Lochlan, Elaina, and Marshall—
my pride, my joy, my love

Hummingbird

# *Prologue*

**M**y name is March Anne Tanner, and I don't know much about rocks. But when I stuck my head out my bedroom window one summer morning, it was for certain sure that I knew about one thing: the color *green*.

That's what growing up on a watermelon farm in Jubilee, Georgia, will do for you. I looked out at the green stretching below our tiny yellow farmhouse. In the front fields, vines were reaching and clawing, crawling and climbing, crisscrossing and curlicuing every which way like a bunch of green snakes rooted in red clay.

Daddy was out there in the fields, as always, with his overalls straining over his pumpkin stomach, making sure the squiggly stripes on the Rattlesnake watermelons were just as squiggly as ever. Making sure that the Jubilee Beauties would ripen to a green as dark and deep as the shadows in cedar trees.

And there was Grenna, my grandma, clattering through the

screen door and stepping out onto the grass below me. My mama died when I was little, so Grenna was kinda like a mom to me. She hooked a hummingbird feeder on the wire hanging from a bracket Daddy had nailed over her bedroom window and squinted up at me with her bright green eyes.

"March Anne," she called. "Pancakes are on the griddle."

On cue, my nine-year-old brother dropped out of the front oak tree and made a beeline for the kitchen.

But I stayed rooted right where I was.

I tossed my red hair over my right shoulder, rubbed my already freckled nose, and kept my own gray-green eyes trained on the summer day outside my window. Just below me, the glimmering jackets of June hummingbirds began glinting in the sun. Dueling and jousting for rights to the feeder, the tiny birds glided effortlessly through the summer air, tilting at each other with their sharp beaks.

Across the way, over beyond the big red barn, clover was gently rising like a low bank of green clouds in the fallow fields where pumpkin vines would grow next year. Beyond those fields, a fringe of trees teepeed into the sky—oak and maple, sweet gum and tulip poplar, hick'ry and loblolly pine.

Down at the end of the long curving drive, a wide curtain of kudzu blocked out the road. Sprawling as big as a stage curtain, it swallowed whole trees, an old pigpen, and even an ancient, rusting Buick in its green. Just last summer, my best friends—Laverne and Meg—and I had watched that kudzu long enough to see it grow before our very eyes.

As I looked out at the Tanner Watermelon Farm stretching

4

below me, I felt certain that this summer would be the same as every other one I'd known. Of course, I didn't know that very shortly I'd start hearing odd things and that something would happen to change my life. Right then all I could think was how my summers were always the same.

*Green, green. Green on green. Green on green on green.*

In fact, Grenna might've said I was taking that summer for *granite*.

Of course, I wouldn't have said that.

I don't know too much about rocks.

*Part One*

*One*

On the last Saturday of June, I heard the seventh whip-poor-will's cry float up from the woods and into my bedroom window. I picked up the phone and called Meg and Laverne, and we planned to meet in the clover field at midnight.

Then I sat down beside the window and looked out at the night throbbing with the chirps and chants of crickets and frogs and katydids. I was turning twelve in August, and I guess I'd lived on a watermelon farm long enough for my blood to pump to the rhythm of all that sound. In fact, nights were so loud outside my bedroom window that every summer I forgot there was such a thing as silence.

But that night I heard another sound above and beyond all the racket. It was the faraway clatter and wail of a train passing by the Point at Sunny Brooke Acres and continuing on through downtown Jubilee. I stared out into the darkness of the fields, wondering where the train was coming from, where it was going.

Suddenly I sat up straighter. The sound of the horn had changed a little. Yes, there it was again. It was almost like a voice calling to me.

"Come . . . come," the voice seemed to cry across the distance.

I stuck my head farther out into the shadows now pinpricked with stars and asked, "Where . . . where?"

Meg and Laverne were already waiting for me in the clover field when I arrived at midnight. Laverne turned on a battery-operated lantern, and wordlessly we started toward the woods.

As we picked our way through briars and branches, Meg was the first to speak. "March Anne, I still don't see why we didn't have our first meeting two weeks ago. Laverne and I told you we've heard a whip-poor-will for two weeks straight at Sunny Brooke Acres." Sunny Brooke was the subdivision of large houses where Meg and Laverne lived.

Meg, who always wears flip-flops—even in winter—was wearing them that night. And I have to admit that the steady slap-slap-slapping into all that dark was kind of comforting. The lantern light splashed onto her pale face, making it shine white like the moon, while her smooth black hair blended into the forest shadows.

"Meg, for the *nine millionth* time, we've got to have our meetings here," I said, tossing my hair behind my shoulder. "These woods are where the Pseudonymphs started, so the seventh whip-poor-will that cries out in *these* woods in June is what signals our summer meeting. Whip-poor-wills are cryin' out from here to Kalamazoo, but the only one that matters to us is the one that cries out *here*."

"I'm sorry, Meg, but I think March Anne is right," Laverne said. As she spoke, the light of the lantern gleamed in her tightly curled blond hair and glanced off the lenses of her glasses. "Besides, there are too many spying eyes in all those houses at Sunny Brooke. The Pseudonymphs would be ruined if one of those obnoxious boys saw us in ritual."

Meg sighed her agreement and trudged on.

Right then we were passing near the cedar tree where a certain hummingbird was snoozing. But we didn't know about the hummingbird then. All we were really thinking about was how dark it was under the canopy of forest leaves.

Finally, we reached the clearing by a special tulip poplar that we had named Maranatha. I'd discovered the tree years ago when I was playing in the woods and had introduced her to Meg and Laverne not long after. We'd immediately seen that she was a *she*, and that she was of royal lineage. We came here to talk and trade secrets or just to sit and think.

This was also our spot for our most solemn Pseudonymph rituals. As Meg's flip-flops finally stopped flopping and flipping, something like quiet seemed to deepen around us despite the trickle of the nearby creek and the continuous chants and chirps.

Meg peered worriedly at the darkness and swatted at a mosquito that seemed to have a particular liking for her left ear.

"Well, Laverne," she said, "can you at least take out the book so we can get started? It's getting kind of creepy out here."

I didn't say anything then, but about that time I thought I saw a shadow move behind a tree about a stone's throw away. I still don't know for sure that there was a shadow. Of course, later that summer, when Daddy told me about the tomatoes and watermelons gone missing, I had my suspicions. But at the time I didn't know any more about the shadow than I did about a great silent owl perched on an oak branch just above us, watching all that was taking place with his ancient, golden eyes. Just then all I knew was that Laverne was pulling the yellow paperback book from her knapsack.

"That's enough of using real names," I said. I was afraid that we might've already said them aloud too many times for the ritual to take.

Laverne placed the yellow book on her knapsack near the lantern. Then we each walked around it in a circle, reverent-like.

We were proud as pumpkins of our first purchase: *Thirty Thousand Names from All Over the World.* We'd sold nine dozen doughnuts at the church social and washed four cars in Sunny Brooke in the spring to raise the funds for it. We hoped to find names for our *future* children by studying the book throughout the next year.

"Now," I said, stopping so suddenly that Meg stepped out of her left flip-flop and Laverne's glasses jostled off the bridge of her nose. Then I spoke the words we'd memorized at the spring Pseudonymph meeting:

"The whip-poor-will cries into the darkness."

"And the darkness gives it back its name," answered Meg and Laverne.

"The whip-poor-will wakes up the katydids of summer."

"Katydids that say their names into the darkness and the light."

"The whip-poor-will wakes up the crickets and the frogs."

"Which also sing their names into the night."

"So we shall say our own names into this darkness. Not the names given us by family nor fate, but our *true* names, the names that find echo in our souls."

We all three looked at the book again. Over the past two years, we'd been Juliet, Isabella, Beatrix, Lilliana, Rosa, and Marlena. Meg's great-great-grandmother was Cherokee, and last summer we'd even tried out Native American names. This year we'd found names within our new book.

Meg was the first to approach the book. She placed her right hand upon the yellow cover and said, "My *real* name has been revealed to me: I am no longer Meg but *Jeanette*. Please take heed." She removed her hand and moved back to her spot in the circle.

"My name," Laverne said, holding one hand on the book and the other on her heart, "my *true* name shall henceforth be *Camilla*."

When Laverne returned to the circle, I fixed my eyes on a

spot where I imagined the whip-poor-will was perched in the darkness. I stepped toward the book and said, "As a Pseudo-nymph, I will now be called *Millicent*."

I returned to my spot in the circle, which, because there were only three of us, was really more of a triangle. Across the darkness, we met eyes and nodded. Then Laverne shouted: "Laverne is now Camilla."

Meg and I shouted back: "Camilla."

"Meg is now Jeanette."

Laverne and I shouted back: "Jeanette."

"March Anne is now Millic——"

Before I could finish my name, the owl overhead decided to answer with its own shouting hoot of a reply, causing us to re-place our calls with high-pitched screams.

I grabbed the lantern.

Meg snatched up the book and knapsack.

And all three of us ran as fast as we could through the dark, damp woods, not caring about twigs that slapped at our cheeks or briars that snatched at our shins.

I imagine it was only when we were out of sight and clear back to the farm that the shadow deep in the woods picked up its heavy burden and started toward home.

*Two*

The next morning, I stared at the water stain on my bedroom ceiling and wondered if Grenna was going wonky in the head. It happened to old people all the time, so why not my grandma?

I could already see the headline in *The Jubilee Neighbor*: OLD WOMAN GOES WONKY IN THE HEAD ON LOCAL WATER-MELON FARM. And, of course, later in the article it would mention the fact that my maternal grandmother had raised me and my little brother, Kevin. Soon after, Kevin would be kicked off his soccer team, which is what he lives for, and I'd be sure to *never* get a boyfriend (not that I wanted one *much* anyway, but it'd been nice to have the option).

My one consolation was that I'd always have Meg and Laverne, no matter what. After the ritual, I'd walked them to the end of the driveway and then snuck back into my bed-room.

I flopped over in my bed, and this time my eyes settled on

the Bible on my bedside table. I didn't read the Good Book much, but that morning I reached over and opened it up to Psalms. That's where I kept my only picture of my mama— right smack-dab in the middle of the whole shebang.

Mama'd died when I was three years old, and with Grenna around, I'd never really missed her too much. But for some reason I kept pulling out the picture this summer—trying to trace myself in her mass of red curls, in her creamy skin, or in the wide brightness of her smile. When I looked long and hard at the picture, something would glimmer deep inside me, and I'd be sure that I'd remember more of her, but I never could retrieve more than a sensation of warmth. And the scent of something like vanilla.

"March Anne, you ready yet?"

Daddy's voice boomed up the stairs. I put the picture back in the Bible, jumped out of bed, and flung open the closet door.

I'd completely forgotten it was Sunday.

Sunday meant only one thing on the Tanner Watermelon Farm: we were going to preaching at Mars Hill Baptist Church. By the time I'd swooped into my dress, shoved on my sandals, and scraped a brush through my hair, Daddy, Kevin, and Grenna were already mashed into the front seat of Daddy's pickup truck. I mashed in, too.

"Better be quicker next time," Daddy said. "You know ol' Comet don't like to be kept waitin'."

I met Daddy's smile with a smile. Comet was the name of Daddy's old pickup truck. She'd been named for her paint, which just happened to be the same green tint as the powder used for scrubbing bathtubs.

I slammed the rusted green door shut, Daddy put Comet in gear, and we eased down the long gravel drive. Fields of watermelon vines stretched out for acres on either side. In fact, if Daddy hadn't kept them cut regular, I was sure those vines would've taken over the driveway completely.

"Comet, Comet, green as vomit," Kevin sang.

"Hush up, grossling," I said to Kevin, reaching across Grenna to pinch his arm as the truck bumped its way over the drive, our hip bones smacking against each other like cued balls on a pool table.

After we turned onto the smooth asphalt road, Grenna touched her silver cloud of hair and started humming hymns. That's what she always did on the way to Sunday services. And though she never sang a word, I always knew the hymns she was humming: "Just As I Am," "Amazing Grace," "The Old Rugged Cross." As she hummed, I sang the words along with her in my head. After all, I hadn't been going to Mars Hill Baptist Church my entire life for nothing.

When preaching was over, we mashed into Comet again. Sunday was Grenna's day off from the kitchen, so we were headed to Burma's Biscuit Barn in downtown Jubilee.

As we left the church parking lot, Daddy flicked on the radio to the station that played the twangy gospel music he liked. That's the way it always was—Grenna humming on the way to church and twangy gospel on the way back home. This time, I was mashed in beside Kevin with Grenna by the truck door.

Just then, Kevin let one fly and hooted to boot.

"Grenna, quick, roll down the window before I gag." I hated to yell over the mournful radio version of "I Surrender All," but it was a needful thing. I pinched Kevin good, but he was laughing so hard that he didn't even notice.

By the time the smell had died down, we'd been over three potholes and crossed the railroad tracks, our hip bones cracking and smacking the whole way like so many more cued pool balls.

Riding down Main Street, we passed the Feed 'n' Seed and First Federal Bank and then the jewelry store and the Red Caboose toy shop before we pulled into a parking space right outside the blue-and-white curtained windows of Burma's Biscuit Barn.

When Grenna wasn't frying chicken, a Burma Bucket was the next best thing. Burma always threw in some coleslaw and biscuits and a gallon of iced tea for free. I think she kind of felt sorry for us since we didn't have a mama.

I'd also seen some of the waitresses making goo-goo eyes at Daddy more than once. But I never saw Daddy do more than nod or tip his baseball cap.

After we were all stuffed, we mashed onto the truck bench yet again.

"Thank you, Bradley," Grenna said to Daddy as she touched her hair.

"Why, you're welcome, Grenna," he said, easing the truck back onto Main Street.

"Comet, Comet, green as vomit," Kevin chanted as twangy gospel music began pouring out of the radio speakers.

The Tanners were on their way home.

Before we got to our driveway, Daddy flicked on Comet's blinker. That meant we were turning at the pine thicket where our family plot is. Grandpap's buried there. So is Mama, and a few other ancient relatives I never knew. Sometimes we just slowed down and kind of looked over toward the pine trees, trying to make out the white stones sticking up out of the ground like huge, misplaced teeth. But other times, like this Sunday, Daddy turned in.

We parked in a little clearing covered with pine straw. Grenna climbed out of the truck and slowly walked over to Grandpap's grave.

Kevin crawled over me and jumped out, too. He started picking up pinecones and putting them in a pile.

Daddy opened his door, slid off the seat, and stood by the side of the truck, watching Grenna.

But I stayed rooted right where I was.

I'd learned a long time ago there wasn't nothing here for me. When I was little, about five years old, I guess, I used to get real excited coming here. I thought I'd get to learn something about Mama. I remember running my hand up and down and across the gravestone, searching for a button that might turn on a screen that showed what Mama looked like or how she sounded. But nothing ever happened. I thumped it. I scraped it. Once I even kicked it. But it didn't move. That old white rock just kept sitting there. Cold, hard, and silent.

Grenna was now walking over to Mama's grave. I thought I heard a snatch of another hymn she was humming. It was weird how Grenna looked so hard at the stone, like she could see something there. Maybe, since she'd known Mama longer than I had, she could.

I looked over at Kevin. He was busy throwing the pine-cones he'd gathered at the squirrels chattering in the branches. Daddy had stayed where he was, leaning against the truck.

No, I didn't know much about Mama, but I knew I'd never learn more about her in this place.

I knew for certain sure I wouldn't learn a thing about her from that old rock.

# Three

$B$ack at home, we all clattered inside the screen door of our farmhouse to see which would win out—the biscuits or the iced tea. See, Burma's biscuits were well-known sleep inducers around Jubilee. But her iced tea, on the other hand, could keep you wide-eyed a month of Sundays. So, although we went back in the house feeling like we wanted a Sunday afternoon nap, chances were we'd end up staring at ceiling stains instead.

Kevin and Daddy made a beeline for the couch and snapped on the TV for a Braves game. Me, I'd rather take my knuckles to a cheese grater. Besides, the lines on our TV were so squiggly that they'd probably see as much baseball if they just set up a Rattlesnake watermelon and took to watching it.

I decided to peek into Grenna's room on my way to the stairs. The smell of face lotion mingled with eucalyptus rub greeted me at her door. Somehow Grenna's room smelled pretty and like medicine and like the woods down near the creek all at the same time. I liked how it smelled.

Grenna was lying on her bed, with her glasses placed neatly on the bedside table and her "tackies"—a collection of trinkets and figurines—sparkling and winking in the afternoon sun on the windowsill. Grenna's eyes were closed, and she seemed to be smiling gently as she snoozed. I guessed the biscuits were winning out for her.

Halfway up the creakity stairs, I knew the tea was definitely winning out for me, so I turned around and opted for the rocker on the front porch instead. I figured it was hotter than Hades in my tiny room by that time of day anyway.

I left Daddy and Kevin doing the Tomahawk Chop as I walked through the screen door into the hot, buzzing day. It was nice to see that Daddy still had *two* eyebrows. Lately it'd seemed like his eyebrows had grown into one big woolly caterpillar under his puckered brow.

I heaved a sigh and plopped down on the rocker. Before Laverne and Meg had left last night, we'd decided to meet later today to ride Spunky. It'd be a while before then, and there was nothing for me to do but wait. I looked out at the front oak and remembered that Laverne was now officially Camilla, Meg was Jeanette, and I was Millicent. I whispered the names into the still, humid air just to hear how good they sounded.

Every time we had a name change, it was confusing to decide when and where we would actually use the new names. We used them primarily in notes or during Pseudonymph meetings. Somehow, though, we all knew that even when we

22

didn't say our official names, we were thinking them. Our new names were mostly a silent understanding between us.

Before I got to rocking in rhythm good, Dorcas jumped into my lap and commenced to purring. Dorcas was our marmalade-colored barn cat. I petted her soft fur while the humid air around me buzzed and whirred and sang and chanted and chirped with a million flying, crawling, hopping, living things. Even Nandina and Shout—an old married couple of redbirds that Grenna had named—were out chirping and flirting in the front oak tree, which housed a hive of bees. The bees were busy buzzing into the blooming fields. No Sunday naps for them in June, but I supposed they would catch up on sleep in December.

As I rocked, I remembered how Grandpap used to rock in the chair beside me. Whittling into the quiet or whistling tunes while Grenna hummed or sang along. That was just four years ago. I kept rocking into the hot, humid, singing air. Almost sleeping, but really staring out into the green and seeing and hearing things I remembered. Almost dreaming, but really remembering the way it had been when Grandpap was alive.

By the time I saw Laverne and Meg starting up the long drive, everybody else was up and at it. Burma's tea had definitely won the day. Kevin was the first to bound out the screen door; he headed to the barn with a soccer ball. Before long he and Spunky, our chestnut-colored mule, were playing soccer with the black-and-white honeycombed ball. It's true, we have what is probably the world's only soccer-playing mule right here on our farm. You'd have to see it to believe it. First, Kevin head-butts the ball up in the air, and then Spunky tosses her head and butts it back. Kevin then passes the ball to her from his left cleat, and, sure enough, Spunk stops the ball with her right hoof, gives a snort, and bats it back to him with her nose. This afternoon they were using the barn door as a goal.

Daddy was next to push open the screen door. "I'm headed to the fields," he said. "I've got two dripper lines down." Our melon fields were irrigated by dripping hoses that kept the soil wet when the rain forgot to. Daddy looked back at me before he headed down the steps, and I couldn't help but notice that his eyebrows had grown into a woolly caterpillar again.

Finally, Grenna sailed out the door with the hummingbird feeder hanging on her finger. She'd cleaned the feeder before church, and now I could see that it was filled with fresh nectar. "Afternoon, March Anne," she said, walking down the porch stairs.

Behind Grenna, Shout was chasing Nandina off an old fence post and taking the roost for his own tufted red self. In a minute, the tawny female redbird returned the favor and settled herself on the post again.

After Grenna climbed back up the porch stairs, she reached out to me. I walked over and put my arm around her and leaned up against her as we both watched the feeder.

It didn't take long before the glimmering jackets of hummingbirds began glinting in the sun once again. Then, suddenly, the motorized birds would pause impossibly still and small at the feeder to take long, watchful drafts of fresh nectar.

"Those birds are the only jewels I've ever wanted in this life," Grenna said. "See how their feathers are made of the rainbows and sunlight and green of a hundred summers?" She was quiet for a minute before she added, "I do declare, March Anne, those little birds could keep a rock from taking this world for granite. Don't you know?"

"Yes, ma'am," I answered.

But I was really thinking how small Grenna suddenly seemed. I'd heard Mrs. Gertrude Mason say once at a church picnic that Grenna was "bird-boned," but I'd never thought of Grenna as small before. After all, she was my grandma.

I'd garnered a mighty big crop of freckles already this summer, but I hadn't noticed until now that it was because my arms and legs had been stretching out so long. The freckles were only keeping up with the new skin.

As Meg and Laverne walked up the drive waving and yelling hello, I saw for the first time that I was a smidgen taller than Grenna. Then, right after a red-vested hummingbird hovered close to our noses before it zigged to the front oak and zagged out of sight, I realized it was Grenna who was now leaning on *me*.

A little later, Meg, Laverne, and I walked through the huge door of the barn as if we were entering another world. Like always, we closed the door, squeezed our eyes shut, and counted to three. That was how long it took for our eyes to adjust to the dark cavern of the barn. Today, when we opened our eyes, the barn was bright in stripes where the June sun forced its yellow between wooden slats and lit upon hay bales and seed tables and wooden beams and stalls. And everywhere, everywhere the dark air was alive with a floating galaxy of silent yellow stars that I suppose were just particles of dust from the hay. But that dark air dancing with gold dust always looked magical and smelled something like Grenna's biscuits baking in the oven. I think we squeezed our eyes shut so we could smell that smell better. Sometimes, when Meg and Laverne and I said "Three" together and opened our eyes to all that dark and gold and quiet, I felt more reverent than I even did at Mars Hill Baptist Church.

"There's Wynken and Blynken, asleep as usual," Meg said, tightening her ponytail.

Laverne adjusted her glasses and peered up to the high beam. "Nod must be out for an early snack."

The white, heart-faced barn owls perched on the rafter like mute, blind valentines. Yet, even in their sleep, they looked wise.

Along with Dorcas, the owls worked to keep our barn mouse-free.

I took Spunky's heavy tack out of the stall, and in a minute, we were back out in the glare and noise and green of the late June afternoon.

By the time we wrestled Spunky away from Kevin and hoisted ourselves onto her back, the sun was sitting above the far fringe of trees. The three of us were mashed into the saddle, and from the front porch of the tiny yellow farmhouse, we must've looked like a leggy centipede as we headed over the clover fields toward the woods. I was at the reins, and right behind me Meg was squeezing her toes white to keep her flip-flops from sliding off. I turned my head and saw Laverne holding on to Meg for dear life, her curls bouncing in rhythm with Spunky's lope.

"I suppose we'll have just enough light left to make it to Maranatha," I said.

"March Anne," Laverne whined, "you said we'd cross the creek and explore some this time."

"Yeah," Meg agreed. "We want to get into that No-Man's-Land that your dad and Grenna are so scared of."

We ducked our heads as Spunky led us through the branches to the path. The trees now arched high and green above us, and, kind of like I had in the barn, I knew for certain sure the feeling I had every time we entered the woods belonged to Sunday.

"I don't know that they're scared exactly," I said, breathing in the smell of old leaves mixed with the freshness of abundant green. "They made up the rule when I was little, probably so I wouldn't wander off too far from the farm."

I glanced back again. Laverne was pushing some stray yellow curls behind her left ear and squinting like she always did when she was thinking hard. "But if we went straight from here and made a path through those woods, all we'd have to do is cross the road and we'd be at Sunny Brooke," she said. "Then we wouldn't have to follow the road like we always do."

"You're forgetting about Crabapple Crutcher," Meg said with some authority. "You know her shack is on the other side of this so-called No-Man's-Land. Grenna was probably trying to keep you out of the claws of that old witch."

"Oh, you know she's not really a witch," I said, as much to myself as to the others. I'd seen the old woman hobbling back into the woods more than once when I'd been on my way to Meg's or Laverne's. One time she'd looked at me with her fierce black eyes, and I'd felt a chill run all the way from my right ear to the tip of my left big toe.

"Well, then," Meg continued, "can you explain how Jim McClendon's new Dalmatian puppy went missing and showed up two days later *without* a tail?"

"Yeah," Laverne agreed. "And right after we had that big downpour last week, Rodney Carver's little sister's kitten disappeared."

I shivered. Every time an animal went missing in Sunny Brooke Acres subdivision, Crabapple Crutcher caught the blame. It was hard to explain how she survived in that shack back in the woods by herself. I'd heard Daddy say that she hadn't been to town in twenty years.

As we rode along the path in the woods, I wondered if it really was time to explore No-Man's-Land. After all, I was almost twelve years old. I wasn't a baby anymore. What was the big deal, anyway?

Without my pulling on the reins, Spunky stopped in a clearing beside the tall, reaching trunk of Maranatha. As usual, the mule had known all along that this was where we were headed.

Just then a shaft of sunlight slanted through the woods and hit smack-dab on Maranatha's white-barked glory. Her leaves, already as broad and flat as lily pads, gently waved hello in the slight stir of evening air. I'd discovered the name Maranatha one day when I was reading the Bible after church. Meg and Laverne had liked the sound of it, although we found out in a dictionary that it wasn't a name, really, but an Aramaic word used as a greeting by early Christians. But that fit, too, as we always felt the welcome of this tall, elegant tree. Under her branches, we always felt something tending to holy.

We'd received many gifts from Maranatha through the years. In the spring, she released tangerine-and-lime-colored poplar tulips to us from her noble arms. In autumn, she gave us our own private ticker-tape parade of a thousand twirly, whirling seeds. And in winter, her sturdy white trunk protected us from the biting north wind as we celebrated our New Year's ritual. A gaping hollow at her roots also housed our deepest secrets, including relics from former Pseudo-nymph rituals, several old diaries, and a piece of paper on which I'd written "March Anne loves Carl Adair" about nine million times—he was a boy I'd had a crush on in the fifth grade, but he'd moved away last year. There was a scoop in the base of Maranatha's trunk that made a perfect nesting spot for me when I came out to visit on my own.

Today we just sat atop Spunky, soaking in Maranatha's summer gifts of green and shade.

The light changed, and the hyena laugh of a woodpecker shouted into the quiet of the woods. As if on cue, I tapped Spunky with my heels and we headed to the creek.

After Spunky had taken a drink, I steered her through the water and we found ourselves in the midst of the cedar thicket.

"I don't know why we're worried about No-Man's-Land." Meg spoke into the shadows that were blending with her dark hair. "Benjamin Hartwell has probably zigzagged across here dozens of times tracking that hawk of his."

"Yeah," Laverne agreed. "The poor boy is at it again this summer. I've seen him crossing through my backyard twice, and yesterday Meg and I spotted him at the Point heading down the train tracks to try to find where that old bird nests."

Spunky had slowed nearly to a stop. She wasn't used to going this far, and she seemed to want to be getting back. I tapped my heels to get her going again, but something zinged through the air right in front of us, causing Spunky to nicker and take three steps back while Meg's flip-flops fell to the ground. Just as suddenly, two birds circled the cedar in front of us. When they circled a second time, I could see they were cardinals. I couldn't tell if they were Nandina and Shout, but in the last of the light I could make out their unmistakable color.

Red.

The color of stop.

\* \* \*

30

By the time we made it back to the farm, lightning bugs were sparking the darkness and yellow light was forcing its way *outside* the slats and loft door of the barn. Daddy had turned on the barn light for us.

Laverne hopped off the saddle and twisted the spigot to water Spunky while Meg jumped down and went to look for the mule's towels and brush.

I unbuckled the saddle and gave Spunky a kiss on the nose. On my way to the stall with the heavy tack, Dorcas scampered down from a high beam and rubbed against my legs. The owls had already flown out into the evening.

As I made my way over to Spunky, I heard a familiar noise rising beyond the evening chants and chirps of the farm. It was the distant roar and moan of the train. Sometimes in the almost-darkness of evening, the train sounded so close, like it was just behind the far fringe of trees and might pop out at any minute and start following watermelon vines instead of tracks.

As the water dripped off Spunky, I heard a voice in the train's moan again. This time it was saying, "Find . . . fiii-innnnd . . ."

I looked at Meg, who was now rubbing Spunky down with a towel. Then I glanced at Laverne, who was busy smoothing out a tangle in Spunky's tail. I could tell that they hadn't heard a thing.

The call, if it was a call, was only for me.

# Four

The next night, after a supper of fried pork chops, string beans, and rice 'n' gravy, Grenna and Daddy sat down to watch the evening news. Or, actually, to *listen* to the evening news and watch squiggly lines. Me, I'd rather have my eyeballs boiled. I hightailed it upstairs to read my latest Nancy Drew.

I came down as they were snapping off the TV. Kevin was in the corner rifling through Grandpap's old records.

"Well, Bradley, that shows you how people will do," Grenna said.

"I know it," Daddy answered, shaking his head. "I wouldn't move to Atlanta for a million bucks."

"What them folks need is to spend some time on a watermelon farm," Grenna said. "Then they'd be too busy to get into such mischief."

"Now that's for certain sure," Daddy said.

Kevin put on a record. Grandpap's ancient record player didn't work too good, and I could never make out all of the words, but I liked listening to the melodies as much as Kevin did. Grandpap had always listened to his records when we played Scrabble, and every once in a while he and Grenna would twirl around on the carpet and dance while Kevin and I watched. Over the years I'd made out enough words to know that the songs were mostly about wartime and missing you and when I see you again and bluebirds. It gave me a nice feeling to know that people sang songs about bluebirds, even if it was a long time ago.

Now the record was playing and the board was in the middle of the table and Grenna's eyes were bright as she was humming and Daddy was cracking peanut shells in his teeth and Kevin was getting the Cokes in little glass bottles from the fridge.

It was time to play Scrabble.

We Tanners played Scrabble almost every Monday night. And, almost every Monday night, Grenna won.

That night was about the same as usual.

Kevin spelled out his first word: DUNG. And then he smiled through the rest of the game like he'd done something to be proud of.

Daddy was also quite pleased with his TRUCK—which racked in 15 points—and later another 19 when he added ING to it.

My three favorite words of the game were GREEN, MID-NIGHT, and CALL.

But Grenna—she came up with the word QUIXOTIC for a whopping 52 points.

"That's not a word!" yelped Kevin, as he always did when Grenna came up with a humdinger.

"Yes, it is, Kevin," I replied like clockwork, even though I'd never heard the funny word before either.

But Kevin still wasn't convinced. He was opening the huge dictionary to make sure.

I'd been playing Scrabble with Grenna long enough to know that if she spelled something out, it was a word. In fact, sometimes I thought that all her wonky talk was just a way of bluffing us so that she could get us good on the Scrabble board.

Then Kevin always found the word, shrugged, and read the definition: "*Quixotic*—to be caught up in the romance of noble deeds, idealistic without regard to practicality."

"Yes," said Grenna, touching her cloud of silver hair. "That's exactly like one of my red-vested hummingbirds, always tilting at the other birds, even Shout, so that a female hummer can take her dainty sips at the feeder."

Tonight, Grenna was definitely *not* wonky in the head.

# Five

*T*wo days after the July Fourth firecracker celebration in downtown Jubilee, Daddy decided it was time to begin pruning. In the morning, we were up at dawn and out in the fields, bending our backs and clipping vines. That way the remaining watermelons would grow big enough to market.

Of course Grenna didn't prune anymore. She stayed inside to make banana sandwiches and put them in the refrigerator so that they'd be nice and cool to eat at noon. Sometimes she added pineapples to the sandwiches at the last minute for a special treat.

Mr. Mack, a neighbor of ours who kept honeybees, always came to help at pruning time. His bees were essential for the proper pollination of our melons. We supplied Mr. Mack with melons in the summer and pumpkins in the fall. Several men from church and a few workers from the Jubilee farmers' co-op also helped. Grenna made sure there was enough iced tea and sandwiches for everyone.

It had rained the night before, so it was blessedly cooler the morning we began. The rain also made the bees slow down a little. All the same, by lunchtime Kevin and I were drenched in sweat and had been stung several times. Our backs also felt like they were about to snap, not to mention our fingers felt broken from pinching the clippers.

That's how it is with work on a farm—you do the same thing over and over until you think either you'll burn up or your back will break. Of course, neither ever happens, and then, just when you think it will never end, Daddy blows a whistle and you know that it's noon.

Today Grenna carried her aluminum folding chair to the middle of the watermelon patch where Kevin and I were working. She had also brought a basket filled with sandwiches and thermoses of iced tea. One thing about working so hard is that you never realize what a blessed thing it is to sit down until you do. I sat on a watermelon the size of a small footstool, and Kevin squatted on one as round as a basketball.

While we ate, Grenna pulled something out of her pocket. She held it up so that we could see it was a watermelon seed.

"Can you imagine, children, how those melons you're sitting on started out as a seed no bigger than a smashed teardrop? Tell me how that happens. Tell me how this little seed will grow to two hundred thousand times its weight."

Kevin and I pondered this as we munched on our cold sandwiches. We knew what was coming next: the Quiz. Every year about pruning time, or sometimes it was harvest, Grenna gave us a Watermelon Quiz.

"When was the first known watermelon harvest?" she asked.

Kevin swallowed his last bite of a pineapple-and-banana sandwich and said promptly, "Five thousand years ago in Egypt."

"When do you plant them?"

I piped up. "After the last spring freeze—usually two weeks after Easter."

"How many pounds of watermelons can be grown on this here farm?"

Kevin sipped his tea and squinted at the far fringe of trees. "Let's see, if a field is irrigated, it can produce thirty thousand pounds an acre. We plant five acres of melons a year, rotating with the fallow, so that's about a hundred and fifty thousand pounds of melon a year."

"Good," Grenna said. "Now, March Anne, how many times does a honeybee have to visit each bloom for it to pollinate?"

I knew this one because she had stumped me with it the year before.

"Ten times to each bloom," I said. "And each bloom stays open only one day, so the bee has to keep really busy to cram all those visits in."

We then looked at the bees crisscrossing in the air above the vines. Without Mr. Mack's next-door honey hives, and the hive in our bee tree, there would be no watermelons.

"You know how this farm started?" Grenna asked.

"With seeds?" Kevin guessed.

"No," Grenna said, her eyes bright, "with rocks."

I frowned and squinted over to her. "Rocks?"

"Yes, March Anne, don't go taking rocks for granite. This farm began with rocks and a dream. You see, a few years after your Grandpap and I were married, we lived in the sweetest little place right near here. We didn't have room to turn around twice, but we were happy there. Anyway, this farm was different then. The timber companies had come in after the war to clear the land around Jubilee and haul the wood out. So here we were with new acres to farm, besides the land that had been my papa's. Now Papa had grown corn and okra for years. But Grandpap wanted to do something different. Of course, he had other dreams once, he wanted to be a railroad man, but after my mama died and Papa took sick and your mama was on the way, he traded it all in for the dream of this place—this watermelon farm. Now, the watermelons weren't enough to keep Grandpap from one of his black moods now and again, but he had a good life.

"That's the way dreams are sometimes," she continued after a short pause. "Kind of like the bees in the watermelon blooms, you got to take what you can get when you can get it.

"So, anyway, with the timber all cleared, we started picking up rocks. We had to get them out of the dirt before we could plant anything. Rocks, rocks, and more rocks." Grenna chuckled as she surveyed the fields. "Yes, our first fine crop was rocks."

"What did you do with them?" I asked.

"Well, child, don't you know? Look underneath the yellow paint at the base of that farmhouse there, and look below the slats of that barn. This farm's built on rocks."

We fell quiet for a minute thinking about this. Then Grenna began staring into the blue sky above the far fringe of trees. She often did this when she came out into the fields. It was almost as if she could see something beyond all that blue, or as if she were reading an old letter written on the puffs of white clouds.

Or maybe, as I suspected, it was one of the ways she was going wonky in the head.

When I looked at her again, though, her eyes were on the edge of the field.

"Look at that white blooming over by the fence. I do believe that's Queen Anne's lace," she said.

We could barely make out the cluster of white flowers that sat like lacy doilies on tall stems.

"Your mama loved that flower," she said.

"Well," said Kevin after he'd drained the last gulp of tea from his thermos, "I think I'll go ride Spunky for a while."

Grenna nodded.

When he was out of earshot she said, "That's his way of looking for her."

I nearly asked "Who?" because it was crazy to look for somebody that was dead. But I stayed quiet because I knew well enough that she meant Mama.

Besides, when I looked back at Grenna, her eyes were already reading something far away in the blue sky again.

* * *

The pruning days all went about the same way. Up at dawn, bending and clipping, then sitting in the fields and eating cold sandwiches and listening to Grenna. Pruning days were like kudzu leaves that way—it was hard to tell where one left off and another began.

Sunday came, and we all mashed into Comet and went to preaching at Mars Hill Baptist Church and took the day off.

Thankfully, it rained that day, and I got to snuggle in the cool of my room with my latest Nancy Drew while Kevin bounced his soccer ball against a wall the livelong day solely to pester me.

But then it was Monday morning, and we were up and out in the fields again.

*Bend, clip, sweat. Sweat, clip, bend.*

That's the way it was from dawn until noon.

Another day Meg and Laverne came to help out. That evening we sat with Grenna on the porch and listened to the whip-poor-will call from the woods while the lightning bugs sparked the darkness of the fields where we'd sweated all morning, and we *knew* what a blessed thing it was to sit down. Dorcas was nestled in Laverne's lap and purring almost as loud as the chirps and chants of the farm.

Kevin was there, too, cracking peanut shells with his teeth.

Later, when it was full dark, Grenna began to rock in her chair and hum the songs about wartime and missing you and bluebirds from Grandpap's old records.

When the moon had risen good enough to make out the dark lumps we knew were watermelons in the fields, and our blood was pumping to the rhythm of the chirps and chants, she started to tell us a story.

"Did I ever tell you about when Grandpap and I got married?"

Kevin and I looked at each other in the moonlight and grinned. She had told us that story many times over the years. But, somehow, there was nothing we wanted to do more at that moment than look out at the night and feel the little bit of coolness in the air and hear that story again.

"It was the sweetest wedding your grandpap and I had," Grenna began. "He'd finally come back from the war, and we couldn't wait to be married. The wedding was in early May, and it was simple, right down in the little Baptist chapel. Simple, but sweet.

"I still had on my white pearls and silk wedding gown when he drove me clear to the train station in Chattanooga. While we waited for the train, we danced to no music whatsoever as I clutched the white roses of my wedding bouquet.

"You see, I didn't know where we were going. Your grandpap had kept it a surprise. Not that it much mattered—I loved him so much and was so glad he'd survived the war that I'd have gone to the moon with him. Grandpap was still in his best suit, smiling and proud as a pumpkin of his new bride.

"I heard the train coming—at first it was a murmur in the distance, not more than the purr of a barn cat at noon. Then the mumble grew as loud as the bees in Mr. Mack's honey hive, and finally, the commotion ripened into a roar.

"The engine was yellow as a butterfly's wing, so I knew that it must be the Yellowbell Express I'd heard tell of in the papers. Oh, she was a beauty, stretched out all silver and gleaming, with a dining car blue as midday.

"We walked down to the sleeper cars. One was as silver as the queen of England's teapot, and around the belly of it was a red band with the word DREAMLINER painted on it.

"Well, I thought I was *dreaming* when your grandpap escorted me over to that very sleeper car. He pushed a button, and the little door fell into a V, and your grandpap held out his hand, and I stepped right up into that *Dreamliner*.

"Imagine, we had the whole car to ourselves. We had a bed and a couch and a table where a waiter brought us food and treated us like the queen and king of the world. And, at that moment, I think we were.

"Well, we rode out of Chattanooga. Clear up and over the mountains of Tennessee. Even further and further up until we reached Virginia.

"And guess what we found there when we stepped off the train? Well, sir, the azaleas were bursting red as the heart of a Jubilee Beauty, and the blooms of the dogwood were unfolding white as wedding veils—exactly like they'd done a month or so before back home.

"Children, we stepped off that train in Virginia and it was spring. *Spring again!*"

When the story ended, I felt like I needed to shut my eyes and count to three. For while Grenna's words had lasted it had been daytime and springtime and somewhere far away. When her words stopped, it took me a minute to readjust to the fact that it was really the middle of summer in the middle of the night in the middle of a watermelon patch in Jubilee, Georgia.

# Six

After the last morning of July pruning, Kevin and I decided to stay outside. He rode Spunky, and I walked alongside as we made our way to the creek. We stomped around in our bare feet for a while looking for crawfish and then headed back home to complete our mission for the day: to dig a hole. Every summer since we were little, Kevin and I had tried to dig our way to China. Of course, we'd known for a few years that this wasn't really possible. I think we kept the tradition going simply because it confirmed the summer freedom to do something for the sole reason that we felt like it. Mostly, I think we liked the powerful feeling of shoveling earth.

When we got back to the barn, we hosed down Spunky, and then we gathered our big shovels and headed to the edge of the field toward Mr. Mack's farm. That's where Grandpap's broken-down black Ford pickup and an ancient claw 'n' ball bathtub roosted in the shade of a huge hick'ry tree. Once used as a watering trough for a milk cow, the tub was now a spa for mosquitoes.

As we reached the spot, Dorcas, who had followed us, perched on the edge of the tub and took a few dainty sips of the greenish water.

Kevin opened the rusted truck door and climbed in and pretended to steer while I stuck my shovel in the ground and plopped the first nice pile of dirt over to the side.

A train started rumbling down the tracks in the distance.

"March Anne, do you ever hear anything in the sound of that train?" Kevin asked.

I stopped digging and stared at him. "You mean a *voice?*" I asked, wild to know if Kevin had heard a call, too.

"No, not a voice exactly," he said, squinting down at the curtain of kudzu at the end of the drive. "More like a notion to go somewhere. To explore. Like out west or something."

"No, I've never heard *exactly* that," I said, choosing my words carefully. "But I have heard *something* in the horn blast of the train a time or two."

After the distant rumble faded away, Kevin slid out of the truck. He left the rusted door open and started digging beside me.

"Do you think Grenna's stories are true?" he asked. "I mean about the rocks and the little place where she and Grandpap lived and the *Dreamliner* and all?"

I was quiet for a minute as the staccato opera of a katydid

filled the air. As I thought about Kevin's question, little snatches of Grenna's stories came back to me:

*We lived in the sweetest little place . . .*

*This farm's built on rocks . . .*

*. . . We stepped off that train in Virginia and it was spring. Spring again!*

"Yes," I said as I felt the sweat starting to trickle down my back. "I suppose her stories are as true as anything else."

Kevin smiled at me.

We returned to our digging, putting our shoulders into it now. After a few minutes, Kevin's shovel clanked on something.

"Look," he said, holding up the hard object like it was the World Cup trophy, "a rock that Grandpap missed."

We both laughed. And kept digging.

Just because it was summer.

Just because we could.


The next day, it happened.

It didn't begin with the blaring whine of the ambulance in the distance and the flashing red lights that seemed to scream even in their silence as they flashed up the driveway. No, that happened more near the end.

The whining scream of the ambulance.

The blaring glare of the red lights.

I knew for certain sure that that blare and scream didn't belong on a watermelon farm, especially not the Tanner Watermelon Farm.

It really began when Kevin discovered Grenna after he'd taken a ride on Spunky. Grenna'd been making her way to the field with her folding chair when she went down. Kevin had run over to her and found that she was unconscious.

Then I heard him yelling.

I dialed 911, and when the lady on the phone asked me what had happened, I didn't know what to tell her, so I just said, "It's my grandma."

Nothing else.

The lady seemed to understand because she didn't ask anything more except our address and phone number.

When she told me the ambulance was on its way, I ran out to the field where Grenna was lying on the ground.

I could tell she was still alive.

That's all.

Daddy came running up from the far edge of the field and let out one deep sob when he saw her. I'd never seen Daddy cry. But I knew his feelings ran deep. Deeper than his words could go.

Daddy reached down, as if he wanted to move Grenna, maybe straighten her out a little, but he took his hand back. He knew we shouldn't move her.

Then came the faraway whine and scream. And the flashing lights up the drive.

That's what I remember most.

Soon after, the ambulance people put Grenna on a stretcher and into the ambulance, and Daddy flew down the gravel drive in Comet right behind them.

Kevin and I stood looking at the empty space they'd left. Looking out over the fields, but not seeing a thing that was green.

Daddy called about two hours later. He said the doctors thought that Grenna had suffered a heart attack. She had regained consciousness and was doing all right, considering what she'd been through, but she was in intensive care, and she was going to need a lot of rest and tests. She would be in the hospital for at least a week, maybe longer.

"Her thinking and her speech may be a little warbled for a while," Daddy said. "They think her heart's suffered some irreparable damage, and she probably won't be too steady on her feet. I'll be home soon to pack up some of her things and then come back to the hospital and spend the night with her."

It rained nearly the whole week that Grenna was in the hospital.

Mrs. Gertrude Mason, a lady about Grenna's age who went to our church, came to stay with us. She was nice enough and made all our meals, but she wasn't Grenna. She spent a lot of time watching soap operas and crocheting.

We went to visit Grenna a few times, and I couldn't bear to see her in that metal bed with those blinking and beeping things hooked up to her. It was good, though, to hear her talk about how sweet the nurses were and to see her even laugh a little when Kevin marched in with a watermelon balloon he had found at Piggly Wiggly.

All week I tried to read my latest Nancy Drew.

I curled up in the hayloft and watched the barn owls snooze.

I pulled the picture of Mama out of the Good Book and traced her mass of curls and bright smile.

I sat on the porch with Kevin and listened to Dorcas purr.

One time, between rain showers, I even walked out to visit Maranatha.

But mostly I stared at the stain on my bedroom ceiling and listened to the rain pour down.

I knew how to translate what the doctors were saying about Grenna. I hadn't been on the sixth-grade honor roll at Jubilee Junior High last year for nothing, after all.

Number one, Grenna was definitely going wonky in the head this time.

Number two, she wouldn't be walking to the middle of the watermelon patch to tell stories anymore.

I also knew something else for certain sure.

Somebody had put a rock smack-dab in the middle of my heart.

# Seven

Finally, Daddy called to say that Grenna was coming home late the next day.

The rain had ended, Kevin had gone to a buddy's house, and it was as hot as Hades in my bedroom, so I gave Meg and Laverne a call. We decided I'd meet up with them at Sunny Brooke, and we'd walk to the Point at noon.

The Point was a big hump in a sloping meadow past the last yard of the last house in Sunny Brooke Acres subdivision. It was a high spot where we could sit and look down at a little valley where Willow Bank Creek wound its way in and out of woods before it turned toward the road. The tiny valley also contained the railroad tracks that curved into Jubilee. So, as often as not, we sat there waiting for a train to come, just for the heck of it.

I shoved on my sneakers, waved goodbye to Mrs. Gertrude Mason, and pushed open the screen door. As it flapped shut behind me, something zinged right in front of my nose—a hummingbird. I waved goodbye to it as well and made my way down the long gravel drive.

I was already sweating when I reached the asphalt road, and I decided to veer a little off my usual course. For some reason I had a notion to pop into the pine thicket and visit the family plot. I guess it was because I had been wondering all week if Grandpap knew what was going on with Grenna.

As I walked toward Grandpap's grave, I was surprised to see something small and white out of the corner of my eye. A bouquet of Queen Anne's lace was lying on the brown, sun-baked pine needles that covered Mama's grave.

I kneeled down and looked at the pretty flowers, wondering who could have left them there.

Suddenly I had a for-certain-sure feeling that someone was watching me.

Slowly, I turned around, scanning the shadows between the pines before I saw Benjamin Hartwell. He seemed as embarrassed at being found there as I was. He lifted his hand in a small wave, and I could tell he was just passing through.

Not knowing what else to do, I reached down and picked up the bouquet. When I looked back again, he was gone.

Back out on the road, I noticed a hawk with its striped wings and fanned-out tail spiraling slowly above the trees in the distance. I figured the bird had unknowingly led Benjamin Hartwell to our family plot.

I passed the stretch of road that bordered Crabapple Crutcher's place. I'd only seen her shack a couple of times, when Meg and Laverne and I had triple-dared one another to go down her dirt driveway far enough to spy on her. Her shack leaned in on itself under an ancient, rusting roof, and it looked ready to cave in at the slightest breeze.

The first time we'd made it back there, we saw Crabapple although she didn't see us. She had seemed harmless enough, shuffling along with her back hunched over and her face wrinkled like a shriveled-up apple. The second time, she'd caught us crouching behind an old wash bin, and she'd took to spitting at us and yelling out of her toothless mouth and chasing us with a broom. That time we'd seen her mean streak up close and personal. We hadn't been back.

There was no sign of Crabapple today, which was just as well. Things seemed creepy enough already.

I looked both ways and crossed the street to Sunny Brooke Acres.

When I rang the doorbell at Meg's house, I thought about how her two-story garage was about the same size as our yellow farmhouse. It seemed strange that only two people—Meg and her mom—lived in such a big house. Meg opened the door with her brush in her hand and a rubber band in her lips.

"Mummph mon min," she said. I followed her into the house while she scooped her smooth black hair into a ponytail at the foyer mirror and expertly looped it into the rubber band.

The air-conditioning in Meg's house washed over my skin and felt heavenly after my long walk. Meg's house always felt comfortable that way, and Laverne's, too—not like the farmhouse, which was always roasting on hot days and freezing on cold.

"I'll get my flips and we'll be ready to flop," Meg called as she ran up the stairs to her room.

As I waited for her, I could hear her mom talking on the phone in the living room. "I told you that you could pick her up at 5:00 on Friday, so why are you pushing the issue?" she said.

*Hmmm,* I thought, *she must be talking to Meg's dad.*

Meg's dad lived in a condominium in Atlanta. Laverne and I had been there a few times on weekends with Meg, and we'd eaten chili dogs and had frosted orange milk shakes at a drive-in restaurant called the Varsity. At night, we slept in sleeping bags in the living room. The living room window looked out over the streets of Atlanta, and I didn't sleep much when I was there. The streets stayed busy long into the night with the beep-beeping of horns and the wailing of sirens. Instead of trees, tall lighted buildings sprouted up from the asphalt in every direction. What really struck me about the night in the city, though, was the sky—it never turned dark but stayed a twilight even at midnight. And the clouds, tinted the same orange color as the milk shakes we'd had, lingered in the air above the buildings all night long.

Meg's mom hung up the phone and went into the kitchen without seeing me. She'd grown up on nearby land here in Jubilee that had once belonged to her Cherokee grandmother, and after college and getting married, she'd come back, somehow wanting to be close to the land where she'd been raised.

Of course, the old farm had been sold and developed into part of Sunny Brooke Acres by then. Meg's dad, though, never could settle into the slower pace of Jubilee. He had to live in the city. Thus, the split.

Meg flip-flopped down the stairs, and we opened the front door.

"Goin' to the Point, Ma," she called into the house.

" 'Kay," her mom yelled back before the door slammed shut.

A few houses down, Laverne's brother Michael came out the front door tossing up a baseball and catching it in a mitt as we walked up the porch stairs. Michael was in high school, so he ignored us. But in the moment that the door was open, we could hear squabbling voices.

"I never said that, you're putting words in my mouth—"

"I don't need to put any words in your mouth, you've already got way too many . . ."

Meg and I looked at each other. The look meant: Ring the doorbell and get her out of there. We acted accordingly.

"Hey, guys," Laverne said after she opened the door. Meg and I said hello as we made our way across the yard.

After the last yard of the last house in the subdivision, we settled down at the Point and hugged our knees to our chests and looked out over the little valley below us without saying anything.

Some people thought the Point an old Cherokee mound—maybe a burial or ceremonial site—but no one really knew. I'd wanted to ask Meg's mom about it more than once, but Meg always shrugged it off. She didn't seem interested in her Cherokee ancestry, although Laverne and I were fascinated by it.

Then we heard it: the distant, rumbling rhythm of the train on the tracks. We'd made it just in time.

We sat and watched the black engine snake its way out of the woods and across the meadow, heading to Jubilee. The rectangular boxcars were black and brown, tawny maroon, and mustard yellow. The colors were comforting and warm— the colors of spices and cocoa, the colors of the layers of dirt when you dig down deep enough, the colors of November leaves.

It was nice to be quiet, especially today, and let our thoughts get swallowed into the roaring sound of the train. By the time the last car had snaked away into the trees, we felt like we'd traveled somewhere in our minds, somewhere away from phone calls and bickering, away from puckered brows and watermelon vines, away from sirens and hospitals.

"Camilla, Jeanette," I said, finally breaking the quiet. "We need to talk."


The evening Grenna arrived home she was determined that everything was going to be the same as before.

We were all determined with her.

Kevin played Grandpap's old records in her bedroom while Daddy and I told her the latest news from church and Jubilee.

The next morning I brought a tray of fruit and tea to her bedroom as she was smoothing pink lotion on her face.

"Good morning," she said, smiling brightly. "I don't be-lieve I've introduced you to my new sidekick, Ellie." Grenna nodded toward the little metal contraption she'd brought home from the hospital.

"No, ma'am," I said, not sure I wanted to be introduced. The thing had ridiculous tennis balls on it for shoes. I knew for certain sure that Grenna had never stepped foot on a ten-nis court in her life.

Grenna laughed a little and told me that she'd named the walker Ellie because it reminded her of a skinny elephant.

While Grenna ate, I picked up a napkin and began dusting the tackies on her windowsill. I had nearly revealed the orange of a ceramic duck's webbed feet when something outside the window caught Grenna's eye.

"March Anne," she said. "Look at the feeder—it's empty. Will you please refill it? The hummingbirds must be starving."

"What do I put in it?" I asked, replacing the duck and peering at the red globe feeder outside.

"Oh, you just warm four cups of water and add one cup of sugar and stir it until it's dissolved," she said. "Just remember, four parts water to one part sugar."

That sounded simple enough.

"And," she called to me, "make sure the mixture cools down before you pour it in the feeder."

I put some water on to warm and popped some bread in the toaster. After all, I was pretty starving myself. I'd spread the butter on the toast when I saw the steam coming off the water and decided I'd better finish the nectar before the water got too hot.

As I poured in the cup of sugar and stirred it with a wooden spoon, something by the refrigerator caught my eye. It was Kevin ducking below the counter. I looked over at my plate. Sure enough, the buttered toast had disappeared.

"You gourd head," I said, running after him. But he'd already made it up the stairs.

I picked up the filled feeder. *Well,* I thought as the screen door slapped shut behind me, *at least that's one thing that hasn't changed—my brother is as pesty as ever.*

# Eight

On Monday, I looked at the calendar and saw we were headed straight-on for the last weekend in July. And the last weekend in July meant one thing in Jubilee, Georgia: it was time for the Watermelon Festival.

That Wednesday, Grenna woke up determined to make her famous watermelon rind pickles. Of course, it was understood that the pickles were also going to win a blue ribbon—just like they had for as long as I could remember.

Meg and Laverne came over to help out. Most folks age their pickles, but Grenna always made hers fresh for the festival. Trouble was only Grenna knew the secret ingredient to make them delicious without the aging.

The screen door swung open, and Daddy walked in carrying a newly ripened Jubilee Beauty. "Fresh from the vine, Grenna, like always," he said.

I couldn't help but notice Daddy's eyebrows were now not only a caterpillar but a sagging caterpillar. All those visits to the hospital and keeping up with the farm had worn him plumb out.

"March Anne," he said, "we've got a few watermelons missing from the vines. A few tomatoes, too. You know anything about that?"

A shadow passed over my memory, but I only shook my head and looked down.

After washing the melon, Daddy started carving the red flesh from the green rind. Kevin jumped to the head of the line for a piece, with Meg, Laverne, and me close behind. It was our first taste of watermelon that summer.

"Wow," I said as the sweet, juicy melon filled my mouth. "Best ever."

Daddy smiled as Laverne, Meg, and Kevin kept going back for more. And we laughed as we tried, unsuccessfully, to keep melon juice from dripping off our chins and onto our T-shirts. Grenna even daintily nibbled a few bites before she turned to the task at hand.

"March Anne, I need the white vinegar from under the sink," she said. "Laverne and Meg, you two look in the cupboard there and get out salt, cloves, gingerroot, and cinnamon sticks. Kevin, get a dozen of the sterilized canning jars from the shelf."

Grenna scooted Ellie over to the sink and began filling two pots with water. While the water flowed out of the faucet, she started humming hymns. I could make out the melody of "At the Cross of Jesus" over the running water.

Grenna hadn't gone to church with us the Sunday before,

and I'd missed her. There'd been no humming of hymns, and without her, the three of us had rattled around in the truck like seeds in a hollowed-out gourd.

"March Anne," she said when the pots were full, "put this pot in the fridge. Kevin, carry this one to the stove for me."

Grenna pushed her tennis-ball-footed contraption over to the stove and flicked on the burner. While she dropped in the freshly skinned rinds, she started humming again. This time it was a wartime song about seeing you again.

As she started combining the spices in a smaller pot, Grenna began telling a story.

"Did you know there was once a queen named Anne?" she asked.

This caught Kevin's attention. "A real queen?"

"Oh yes, child," Grenna said. "Over in England. That's who them white flowers out at the edge of the field are named after. Now there's some as call those flowers 'common carrot,' though I never did. It makes a world of difference, what you call things, don't you think?" She looked up for a moment and winked a green eye at Meg.

Meg nodded, and Grenna continued measuring and pouring and stirring—and telling.

"You know," she said, turning her eyes toward me, "your mama planned her wedding around that flower."

I looked down at the spices swirling together in the pot.

"Oh, yes, she loved this land," Grenna continued as she stirred. "She was always running barefoot out across the fields, like you girls. Keeping her in the house on a blue day was like trying to keep Spunky trapped in the stall before suppertime. So I opened the door and let her go.

"Well, after she met your daddy, they were soon engaged. And when we asked her when the wedding was, she said, 'Mama, it's whenever the first lace blooms in the meadow.'

"So she didn't set a date, but every day that summer she walked to the meadow. One day she walked in and said, 'Mama, get the dress out of the trunk and call the preacher— I'm getting married today.'

"We gathered down at the meadow right before sunset, and I tell you, child, I've been to many weddings, but this was the prettiest by far. You see, there weren't no walls—just trees and sky and air and birdsong. Your mama came out of the woods with her arm laced up in Grandpap's and with a smile glowing on her face. She didn't hold any flowers in her arms— she didn't need to—she was wading into a sea of flowers, a cathedral of Queen Anne's lace!

"She had on my silk wedding gown, and she was wearing my mother's pearls, but no one took notice of nothing but those pretty flowers and that smile. Yes, ma'am, it was the prettiest wedding I ever saw."

Then Grenna fell to humming again and singing in snatches.

On Friday, Meg, Laverne, and I took a jaunt on Spunky. During our ride, we discussed our idea for a popcorn booth at the Watermelon Festival. All that talk made us hungry.

When we got back, Kevin offered to hose down Spunky, so we made a beeline to the kitchen. There, on the counter, were the little jars of watermelon rind pickles lined up in the late afternoon sunshine. The pickles looked beautiful as they sparkled in the glass jars with golden lids. Grenna had tied a red-checked bow around the jar to be entered into the contest. The golden jars reminded me of the pumpkin preserves Grenna was also famous for around Jubilee. She always made some for the Tanner Pumpkin Patch in October.

As I pulled the popcorn out of the cupboard, I turned to my friends. They were both spending the night so that we could go to the festival together the next day.

"Camilla," I said to Laverne, "we spent our whole Wednesday morning here in the kitchen with Grenna. Do you have the faintest notion of how to make these pickles?"

"Umm, take a watermelon and chop it up," she said as she mashed a curl behind her ear and squinted. "And add . . . some cinnamon?"

"Jeanette, what about you?"

"Add vinegar . . . and salt . . . and sugar, and heat it all up?" Meg replied before she shrugged and gave up. Then she asked, "What about you, Millicent?"

I poured the popcorn into the air popper and turned to them again, laughing. "Girls, the truth be known, I've no more idea of how to make those pickles than how to send Dorcas to Mars."

"You girls ready yet?" Daddy's voice boomed up to us.

Laverne, Meg, and I grabbed our things and bounded down the stairs.

Grenna was tired from the pickle making, so she was still in bed. We yelled goodbye to her and mashed into Comet. Kevin rode in the back so he could make sure Daddy's prize watermelons didn't get banged around too much. An air popper, popcorn, salt shaker, and bags were also packed up in a box for our Pseudonymph booth.

Daddy flicked on the radio to the honky-tonk music and eased Comet down the driveway in between fields of vines boasting watermelons as big as year-old pigs.

We were on our way to the Jubilee Watermelon Festival.

As we pulled up to the fairgrounds, we rolled down the truck window and Daddy turned off the radio. The first thing we saw was the Ferris wheel spinning against the blue sky. I could barely hear a melody cranking out from the carousel just before more honky-tonk music poured from the speakers mounted on poles in the parking lot.

We piled out of Comet and went our separate ways. Daddy had to haul his watermelons over to enter them officially into the festival, and Kevin and Laverne were going to sign up for the watermelon seed spitting contest. Laverne came from a long line of champion women spitters, and she was going to do her best to keep the trophy in the family. Meg and I were going to enter Grenna's rind pickles into the food contest and then set up the popcorn booth for later in the afternoon.

As we made our way past a booth selling sausages and cotton candy, I asked Meg if she was going to enter the Jubilee Beauty Contest. I thought she'd make a lovely queen, with her creamy skin and black silken hair.

"March Anne, you know I'm not the beauty contest type," she said, flicking her ponytail in defiance. "Besides," she added, "nobody stands a chance against Colette Violetti."

As if on cue, Colette Violetti sashayed from around the corner of the Alpine roller coaster, her long blond hair gleaming in the sun. She was the only girl going into the seventh grade at Jubilee Junior High who had any excuse for wearing a bra. And she knew it. She didn't even look our way.

When we met up at the Jubilee Beauty Contest, Daddy's own Jubilee Beauty watermelon had already won Best of Festival, and Laverne had spit her way into a picture sure to make the first page of *The Jubilee Neighbor*. Kevin, who hadn't placed, gazed at her trophy in awe.

We took our places in the crowd gathered at the stage and munched on candied apples as we waited for the contest to begin.

"Oh, gag," Meg said, "it's the boys from Sunny Brooke."

I searched the crowd for Benjamin Hartwell's brown hair. There he was, shoving an enormous hot dog into his mouth. His friend Jim McClendon, who, by the way, always kept his hair in a crew cut, even in winter, was with him. Jim was busy yanking a new yo-yo he'd won at some game booth. Beside Jim stood sandy-haired Rodney Carver sucking down a huge lemonade.

"I heard they've set up a booth right across from ours," Laverne said.

"Yeah," Kevin chimed in, "they're taking bids for *swallowing* tadpoles. I heard that someone offered Rodney Carver fifty bucks to gulp down a dozen of the little black squirmers."

Meg, Laverne, and I looked at one another, our apples already turning in our stomachs, and said one word. *"Gross."*

It didn't take long before Colette Violetti's name was announced as the Jubilee Beauty.

Benjamin Hartwell let out a whistle loud enough to wake up the cows in Kalamazoo.

I rolled my eyes.

Jim McClendon rubbed his crew cut and cheered.

Meg puckered her lips like she was sucking on something sour.

Rodney Carver tossed his sandy head and howled with delight.

Laverne flared her nostrils and picked up her trophy.

Colette had been crowned.

The Pseudonymphs were ready to pop some corn.

It turned out that the Sunny Brooke boys' booth *was* across from ours.

Thankfully, it also turned out that the boys were not *swallowing* tadpoles—they were merely selling them. They had caught the tadpoles at the creek and put them in little jars, and they were selling them for a dollar apiece. As a small line of children formed at their booth, I wondered what the boys were going to do with their money. We were going to use ours to buy one another silver charm necklaces around Christmastime.

Meg peered at Jim McClendon like he was a beetle. "I'm afraid that tadpole booth is going to kill our business. No one will want to eat popcorn after seeing those slimy things in jars."

I glanced over at Benjamin Hartwell, who was looking back at us with his dark brown eyes. Was he snickering at our defeat?

Fortunately, as Laverne was salting the second batch of corn and Meg and I were bagging it, a small line began to form at our booth. I guess we'd finally popped enough for the smell of fresh corn to fill the air. Soon we were popping and bagging and taking quarters so fast that we didn't even notice that the Sunny Brooke boys were next in line.

"So, girls," Jim McClendon said, grabbing a bag of corn, "where are the *proceeds* from this popcorn going?"

Rodney Carver pulled a crumpled dollar out of his jeans pocket and placed it on the table. "Yeah," he said, "I've heard tell that you girls belong to some kind of *club*."

Benjamin Hartwell crossed his arms and waited for our answer.

"Well," Meg piped up, "maybe we'll tell you all about it

when you tell us what y'all are doing with your tadpole money."

Jim McClendon rubbed his crew cut.

Rodney Carver started to whistle.

And Benjamin Hartwell shifted his eyes to the Ferris wheel, which was now brightly spoked with yellow and blue lights against the darkening sky.

"I think y'all better mind your own business," I said, nodding across the way. I had noticed a crowd looking at the jars of tadpoles.

The boys didn't waste any time hustling back to their booth.

Before we left the festival, Meg, Laverne, and I mashed into a seat on the Ferris wheel and rode up toward the sliver of silver moon.

Jim McClendon, Rodney Carver, and Benjamin Hartwell were each riding solo on the three consecutive seats behind us, hooting and howling like so many monkeys at the Atlanta zoo.

In many ways it had been a grand day at the Jubilee Watermelon Festival. We'd made twenty-eight dollars and fifty cents selling popcorn. It was even kind of comforting to know that Colette Violetti had won the beauty contest as we knew she would.

But every time we rode up into the star-sparked sky, I felt like I'd left my heart back down on the dust of the fairgrounds. I couldn't get Grenna's pickles off my mind.

Earlier, after we'd closed the popcorn booth, I'd run over to the food contest tables to see how the watermelon rind pickles had fared. There sat Grenna's pickles, without a blue ribbon. In fact, besides the red-checked ribbon Grenna had tied around the jar herself, there was no other ribbon at all.

I opened the jar as Kevin reached the table. I took a bite and winced.

The pickles were too salty and too sour.

And they weren't a bit sweet.

After we dropped Meg and Laverne home at Sunny Brooke, I kept wondering how we were going to break the news to Grenna. Kevin was slapping his thigh in time with the honky-tonk music as we rode up the driveway, but I could tell he was wondering the same thing. I hoped Grenna had gone to bed early, but when Comet pulled up beside the farmhouse, I could see a light still on in the living room. She was waiting for us.

I slowly opened the screen door with the air popper in one hand and the jar of pickles in the other. Kevin was behind me, with Daddy bringing up the rear. Then I saw Kevin zig toward Daddy and zag back toward me and grab the jar. Before I could say a word, he started jamming the jar and Daddy's blue ribbon up under Grenna's nose.

"You won," Kevin yelped. "Best of Fair! Your pickles won again!"

Grenna's eyes grew a touch brighter in the lamplight with what I thought must be tears. She hugged Kevin and said,

"Well, honey, as long as I always win a blue ribbon with you, that's all I care about." She held Kevin in a bear hug as she looked over his shoulder at Daddy and then at me and smiled.

As I made my way up the creakity stairs that night, I suspected Grenna knew she hadn't won the blue ribbon. And it didn't really matter to her. Kevin's hug was her prize.

She may have been a little wonky in the head, but, despite what the doctors said, I knew there wasn't a thing wrong with her heart.

# Nine

A few weeks later I woke up and looked over at the decoupage snail Grenna had made for me. On the bottom it read: "The biggest dreams live in the smallest houses." That was one of Grenna's famous sayings. I put the snail back on my bedside table and sighed.

Today was August 17th, my birthday, and I was as stumped as ever about one thing: my name.

I knew that March was Grandpap's last name, but how could I be named *March* when I was born in *August*? Twelve years old, and I was still perplexed by my name. It just didn't seem right to be born in one month and named for another.

Something was rotten in the state of Georgia. Something wasn't jiving in Jubilee.

Now, *Augusta* was a name I liked. It had some romance—some *ummph*, some *mystery* to it. But *March* was short and choppy, to the point, beside the point. And to be coupled with *Anne*—bland *Anne*—a name repeated in my last name—*Tan-*

*ner*—made the name the height of triteness. My one consolation was that, at least where Jeanette and Camilla were concerned, I was Millicent this summer.

I peered up at the stain on my ceiling. Something else was bothering me. Everyone was acting like Grenna hadn't had a heart attack. When it was for certain sure that she had.

The telltale signs were everywhere.

For one thing, Kevin and I were always making trays of salt-free, fat-free food and bringing them into Grenna's bedroom. She was the one who had always served us before.

Second, a string of women from the church kept lining up at the door with casseroles for us to eat and cards or flowers for Grenna. Of course, every one of them was making goo-goo eyes at Daddy.

Thank goodness all he ever did was nod or tip his baseball cap and escape back into the fields.

But that was another thing. The watermelons were ripe, and it had always been Grenna who'd inspected the melons to give the official call to begin harvest.

Then, yesterday, as we sat on the front porch watching hummingbirds, she'd given the job to me.

After my bowl of cornflakes, I walked out into the first field. A morning glory vine was twisting into the melon vines and blooming as bright and blue as the sky at noon. The bees were already busy. Nandina and Shout were out, too, twittering at me and urging me on in my task.

I'd watched Grenna check the melons for ripeness since I

was four years old. I knew what she did, but I didn't know if I could do it myself.

I looked around at the hundreds of melons rising like small whales in a sea of green leaves and wondered where to begin.

*You were born right smack-dab in the middle of watermelon harvest,* I could hear Grenna say in my mind. *You grew ripe right along with those melons.*

I scanned the first patch of vines.

*First, check the vine tendrils closest to the melon to see if they're curly and brown,* Grenna had always told me. I kneeled down to see the tendrils tightly wound and the color of the bark on pine trees. In my mind I could also hear Grenna say, *March Anne, your red hair learned its curl from those melon tendrils. You grew up right along those rows of vines.*

I walked to the second patch. *Thump the melons, March Anne. They should sound as hollow as a gourd.* I thumped a few. I knew the sound well. These melons had been my first and only drums when I was a small child. In early July, the sound of a Jubilee Beauty was tinny, almost as if I were hitting Comet's hood. But now, in mid-August, the sound was deeper somehow, as if I were slapping a soccer ball.

I picked my way farther down to the next field.

*Rub the melons, March Anne. When you can feel the slightest little ridges along the stripes, you'll know they're ripe.* I ran my fingers across the squiggly dark and light stripes of a Rattlesnake watermelon, and sure enough, I could feel the little lined indentations.

In the next patch I pondered the dark, brooding Moon 'n'

Stars watermelons. *Look at the blossom end, March Anne; if the North Star is peeking out, then they're ready to pick.* I crouched down and saw how, besides the whitish-yellowish constellation of dots on the dark, almost black melon, a star was bursting out at the bloom end of the melon.

Then I turned over the next melon on the vine to inspect the spot where it had lain on the ground. *Only when that ground spot is as yellow as the noonday sun, March Anne, are the melons red as a sunset inside.* The ground spot was as yellow as a butterfly's wing.

Most of the things that happened that day were like my other birthdays. I still lived in the tiny yellow house. I was still perplexed by my name.

Other things were different, though, like the uninvited Ellie at the table when I opened my presents. And the fact that my birthday cake was from the Piggly Wiggly bakery instead of being made from scratch by Grenna.

But my best friends and my family were still around the table in the kitchen, smiling at me, wishing me well, and raising their voices together in song—and those were the most important things, after all.

Maybe it was because of the blaring red siren that had seemed to change everything.

Maybe it was because I knew that summer was winding down and I wanted to savor the sweet last bit of it.

Or maybe it was because we had been harvesting watermelons for over a week, bending our backs and cutting stems so the men could load the heavy melons onto the trucks, day in and day out, and I was plain exhausted.

But for whatever reason that August night, as I sat by my open bedroom window, I felt the deep quiet of things beyond the regular chants and chirps of the farm.

I didn't hear the train that night, but I could hear a call in the quiet just the same.

Telling me to come. Telling me to find.

I returned the hazy gaze of moon and wondered *where* it was I was supposed to arrive.

I watched the telling bellies of lightning bugs. If I could only figure out their yellow code, I thought, I'd know *what* it was I needed to find.

I looked out at the trees and vines I knew were green even though I couldn't see the color now. I could *feel* the greenness, feel the growing and breathing of green in the dark. Peering out over the fields, I asked the night *who* was calling me.

I didn't hear any answer, but I stayed rooted right where I was until that quiet would no longer allow me to deny what I'd known deep down all along.

It was Mama.

Part Two

# Ten

"What was that?" Laverne asked when Meg's trowel clinked on something in the dirt where she was digging holes for hyacinths.

"Probably a rock," I said as I continued mixing bonemeal into the soil for a cluster of crocuses.

It was the second Friday in September, and we'd met at my house after school to walk to Maranatha and plant spring bulbs in the small clearing at her roots. Grenna and I had ordered the bulbs from a seed catalog the last week in August.

Today the air was cool and breezy, and without the heavy humidity that hangs over Jubilee all summer, the bright blue of the sky seemed very far above Maranatha's branches. Even the frenzied chirps of the crickets seemed to have slowed a little.

After I'd dug for a while, I grabbed a daffodil bulb and shoved it down into the hole I'd made. The bulb looked as ugly as a shriveled onion, and it was hard to imagine the frilled yellow flower hiding somewhere deep inside it.

As we worked, Meg and Laverne chatted about school. But my mind kept returning to past Pseudonymph rituals that had been performed on the very clearing where we were now digging. Like the time we'd each cut off two inches of one another's hair (only an inch and a half of Laverne's because her hair was rather short that year) and scattered it for the birds to gather to line their nests. Another time we'd punctured our thumbs with the sharp tip of a pinecone and pressed the tiny red beads of blood on each other's thumbs together to become "blood sisters."

Meg's trowel clinked again, and the noise was somehow clinkier than when a trowel hits a rock. It wasn't a normal digging sound.

Laverne and I scooted over for further investigation. Meg was uncovering a few inches of smooth, dark metal. We dug beside her—me on one side and Laverne on the other. Yes, the metal was about two inches wide and it continued in both directions. It looked to be part of a railroad track.

"Let's see if the other rail is here," Meg said.

After a few more minutes of digging, we found the matching rail. It was definitely a train track. We decided to plant the rest of our bulbs in the middle of the two rails to commemorate our discovery.

As I planted the last crocus, I thought about how much time I'd spent at Maranatha without knowing what was hiding right there under the soil near her feet. Laverne took out our official Pseudonymph book, and she and Meg started researching fall names while I stretched my back and gazed up at the branches that were a flutter of restless green in the breezy air above me. While they debated the merits of Angelica and Penelope, I walked over and lay down, looking up at Maranatha's wide canopy of leaves.

"You knew about this the whole time, didn't you?" I whispered.

The distant rumble of a train sounded from the distance.

Behind me, Meg laughed as Laverne joked that we should go for the names Helga, Hulga, and Ursula at our next name change. We wouldn't do an official ritual until Maranatha began to release her twirly seeds and it actually *felt* like fall.

When the train whistled its moaning cry, I knew that the call was still there. But this time the word had changed again. In the last few blasts I finally made it out: "Dream . . . dreeeeam . . . dreeeeeeeeeeam . . ."

Lingering another moment, I silently asked the blue sky, *How . . . how?*

*L*ike most kids who live in Jubilee, I walked to the end of my driveway to catch the school bus. But unlike those of most kids, my driveway was about half a mile long—so I couldn't afford to be late coming out of the house or I'd miss the bus altogether.

As I started down the driveway through that crisp early Monday morning, Nandina and Shout were already flitting and flirting in the front oak. I thought back to the day when Grenna had named the female cardinal after the little tawny red berries that grow on the bushes beside our porch. She'd named the male bird after the holly berries that "shout" red into winter.

Farther on, bright purple morning glories were blooming amid one or two straggling watermelons in the field beside the driveway. Daddy had told me the night before that someone had been clipping the unharvested melons off the vines in the past few weeks, and I'd wondered if the Sunny Brooke boys were up to more pranks. Near the end of the driveway, just before the curtain of kudzu, late-blooming honeysuckle trumpeted out from a patch of small orange pumpkins.

When I reached the road, I heard the distant churning engine and the grind of gears. Then I saw the yellow school bus cresting the hill. It had just come from Sunny Brooke Acres. Laverne and Meg would be onboard to greet me, which was good. Benjamin Hartwell, Jim McClendon, and Rodney Carver would be sitting in the back, which was not good. Worst of all, it meant Colette Violetti—the blond, blue-eyed Jubilee Beauty of the Watermelon Festival—would be sitting pretty in her plaid skirt, turtleneck, and knee-highs.

The bus stopped, the door fell into a V, and I stepped up onto the stairs. As I scanned the seats for Meg and Laverne, Colette smiled a row of perfect teeth, but, as usual, she didn't scoot over to make room for me to sit with her. I smiled back, still scanning. Then Benjamin Hartwell poked his head out from behind a seat at the back of the bus with his eyelids peeled backward. Jim McClendon and Rodney Carver chortled and guffawed.

Finally, I saw my two best buddies on the hump seat. I waved hello and sat down. We were on our way to Jubilee Junior High.

Monday morning had officially begun.

"We opened the door and *influenza*," Mr. Farkle said, leaping up from his desk as I walked into science class.

Mr. Farkle, my science teacher, was a bushy-haired, bushy-bearded man who hopped around the room like he had too much helium in his back pocket.

I smiled and hurried through the doorway to find my own desk as Mr. Farkle continued to chant, "Give me microscopes, give me petri dishes, or give me tests!"

My favorite subject at school was science. Of course, I liked Mrs. Rulanger, my new English teacher, well enough, and Mr. Jenkins, my P.E. coach, but science as a subject was my first love. And with science came Mr. Farkle.

What I loved about him was that he *loved* science. He recited the periodic table of elements with the same awe and respect with which a soldier recites the Pledge of Allegiance.

What I didn't like about science class were the boys.

I'd thought seventh grade might be a little different where boys were concerned. Then I had to sit beside Benjamin Hartwell.

Now, as I mentioned before, Benjamin had dark brown eyes. In fact, in those first days of school, it occurred to me that his eyes were the color of melted chocolate. But, despite the eyes, I found out that boys hadn't changed much since the sixth grade.

Take the first week of school, when we'd been studying the frog's life cycle, for example. We'd just been looking at a jar of tadpoles when Benjamin opened his mouth. On his tongue was some kind of slimy, stretchy toy frog. Rodney Carver and Jim McClendon thought this was the most hilarious thing since the day the rubber eye popped out of Mr. Farkle's skeleton model and landed in his coffee mug.

Meg, Laverne, and I met eyes and rolled them.

I had one word to say: *Weird*. My only consolation was that we got to choose our partners for the fall research project. Meg, Laverne, and I were hoping to work as a threesome. Then we would finally get away from the boys and do some serious science.

Meanwhile, Mr. Farkle was hopping around from one desk to the next. "To market, to market, to buy a fat frog, home again, home again, jiggety jog."

On another day, we watched a video on the parts of a heart. Benjamin pulled out a rubber pig's snout and wore it through the video.

*Weird*.

Mr. Farkle stopped by our table. "Give me heart chambers or give me tests!"

Today we were analyzing owl pellets. I was especially interested in this experiment because of our barn owls. But, for some reason, Benjamin thought the analysis needed the sound effects of a whoopee cushion.

*Weird*.

Meanwhile, Mr. Farkle was staring up at the periodic table of elements and singing, ". . . put 'em together and what have you got? A cure for cancer and flu!"

No, seventh grade hadn't changed the boys a bit. I wondered if and when seventh grade would change me.

* * *

"Watermelons are going for sixty-nine cents a pound," Daddy announced from the kitchen as the screen door slapped behind me after school.

"Hmmm," I said, plopping down my backpack and reaching for a huge Granny Smith apple on the counter.

Kevin suddenly appeared from behind the counter and grabbed the apple I was reaching for, then disappeared again.

"Melon head," I called after him.

I chose one of the smaller apples and looked at my dad.

I'd found Daddy like this more and more lately—squinting at the grocery prices in the Piggly Wiggly flyer with his face all squished like he'd just taken a bite of watermelon too close to the rind.

I knew Daddy wasn't looking at the grocery flyer because he was interested in buying watermelons. For, as Jubilee folk would say, we Tanners had watermelons coming out the wazoo. But Daddy was interested in the price of watermelons. He'd already gotten his price for this year's crop, but he was researching how much he should sell for at the farmers' market next year.

"Would you look at this?" he said, pointing to the flyer. "Milk for three ninety-nine, and eggs over a dollar a dozen. I knew we should've kept that milk cow and those chickens!"

My dad didn't blink twice at digging and planting his own food in mud and manure, but he'd always been jittery about pushing a cart up and down air-conditioned grocery store aisles. Of course, Grenna had done the food shopping for years, but since Grenna's heart attack, Daddy'd taken over the task.

"I do declare," he said, his squinting eyes now directed out the window toward the far fringe of trees. "It's getting harder and harder to make ends meet."

I knew that, besides our money from crops, Daddy, like many independent farmers, got some government money. But it never seemed to be enough. He'd talked about adding a third crop, but he was afraid that the year-round planting in the same fields might leave the dirt good for nothing but fire ants.

Daddy rubbed his caterpillar brows and looked at me. "By the way, March Anne, one or two of the young pumpkins have gone missing lately. I just can't figure it out," he said.

I took a chomp out of my apple, which was both wonderfully sour and sweet at the same time. "Well," I said between bites. "Maybe the raccoons have taken to weight lifting and are bulking up to try out for the football team."

Daddy chuckled and said, "I've been meaning to tell you, too, March Anne. It's high time you took more responsibility in the food department since Grenna's not feeling herself. Starting this week, you'll be cooking dinner."

*Cooking? Dinner?*

I looked at my apple. Somehow it now appeared more sour than sweet.

Either that or I'd just lost my appetite.

* * *

About a week later, I heard a racket loud enough to curl the yellow paint off the farmhouse.

*Slam! Slap! Whap!*

I poked my head out the bedroom window and saw the black-and-white soccer ball sail up from the toe of Kevin's cleat, slam into the slats of the huge red barn, and bounce back to him again.

Kevin trained his eyes on the closed barn door and kicked the ball again. *Slam!*

Soccer season was gearing up, with almost daily practices and scrimmages, but this was ridiculous. The racket was giving me a migraine the size of a Moon 'n' Stars watermelon.

"What are you trying to do?" I called out to him. "Make like Snap, Crackle, and Pop for little green people on Mars?"

"Nah," he called back up to me. "Just tryin' to wake up them lazy ol' barn owls."

Kevin was always playing pranks on Wynken, Blynken, and Nod. I'd named the owls, and I was pretty sure my brother didn't like the names. In fact, now that he was nine, I was pretty sure he didn't even like the owls anymore.

I looked out to where the old mule was grazing peacefully in the pasture. I'd suspected that Kevin wouldn't have been kicking the ball so hard if Spunky had been in her stall.

*Wa-boom! Whap! Slam!*

"All they ever do is sit on that top rail with their droopy eyes in their heartsy-fartsy faces," Kevin yelled up to me between kicks. "It's time for them to wake up good. I want to see 'em fly during the day!"

I pulled my head back in the window and bounded down the stairs. I slowed at Grenna's door and looked in. By some miracle, she was napping blissfully despite the racket.

*Boom! Ba-boom! Slam!*

On the porch, I saw Dorcas squeezing out of a hole in the foundation of the barn. She arched her back in a tall stretch punctuated by a lazy yawn. Kevin's kicking had definitely disturbed her afternoon slumber in the hayloft.

I shook my head at my brother, opened the huge barn door, and stepped inside. The sound of Kevin's kicking echoed through the rafters, causing a blizzard of hay specks to fly wildly through the air. I peered up through the light-slanted shadows and saw that Wynken, Blynken, and Nod, like Grenna, were still sound asleep.

*Wa-boom! Whack! Crash!*

Back outside the barn, I turned toward the far meadow. I was thinking about a walk to the woods. But I stopped myself.

Dinner.

I'd promised Daddy I'd make it that night.

As Kevin continued his kicking frenzy, I went back into the house and headed for the kitchen. I didn't have the heart to wake Grenna, so I'd have to face the kitchen alone.

When I opened the refrigerator, my stomach turned. The fallout from several days' worth of cooking disasters was sitting there in Tupperware containers.

Small green bowl: a steak charred blacker than the asphalt at Carson's Cars for Less.

That night, Daddy had simply smiled and walked over to

the kitchen drawer, pulled out the can opener, and opened a can of pork and beans.

Pink rectangular dish: a yellowish liquid with little black particles roughly the size and texture of tadpoles swimming in it. This had been my attempt at gravy.

That night, canned field peas.

Large yellow tub: what I'd hoped to be a masterpiece—chicken pot pie. I had followed the directions exactly—well, *too exactly* as it turned out. The recipe had read: Add boiled chicken, boiled egg, cream of mushroom soup, carrots, and peas. Cover with a pastry crust and bake at 375 degrees for thirty minutes or until crust is golden brown.

When Daddy cut into the pastry crust, which was actually a beautiful golden brown, he was quite surprised to see a whole chicken floating beside two eggs—still in the shells—with two whole carrots and quite a bit of peas and soup for broth. Of course, the fact that the pastry was put over the aluminum boiling pot instead of the baking pan should have been his first clue.

But, once again, Daddy only laughed. "I remember your mother telling me she did the same thing when she first tried chicken pot pie," he said.

That night, pinto beans.

Kevin, on the other hand, didn't think the mishmash pie was so funny. I had to admit, the canned beans Daddy'd been heating up weren't really satisfying.

And that wasn't even considering the gastrointestinal effects. I'd noticed a wretched odor hovering inside our small house. I'd calculated that the methane gas buildup in Kevin's room alone could cause a spontaneous combustion at the slightest spark. I, for one, had started sleeping with the window cracked.

*Whack! Slam! Kaboom!*

*Poor pesky little fellow,* I said to myself. *He's probably working off frustrations.*

*I know. I'll whip him up some biscuits. Just like the ones Grenna used to make. That'll cheer him up.*

I pulled the bag of flour down from the cupboard and set to work.

"I'm not eatin' that," Kevin announced when he sat down at the kitchen table. He was eyeing the speckled concoction that had been my attempt at green bean casserole.

"Suit yourself," Daddy said. "It looks pretty good to me."

I had to admit I wasn't sure if I was up to a taste of it myself.

"Here," I said, passing the basket of golden brown biscuits to Kevin.

He looked at the biscuits and then back at me.

They were beautiful.

My first culinary triumph.

I watched Kevin take the first bite.

Instead of the smile I'd expected, he yowled instead.

"My tooth! My front tooth! That hockey puck of a piece of crud almost chipped it off!" he yelled.

"Dork brain," I said. Then I tried a bite, only to find that he was right. The biscuits were harder than hick'ry nut shells. But I was still raw at his words.

"I'd like to see you do better," I said. "Anything you'd cook would probably taste like it had been scraped from the bottom of Spunky's stall."

"Children, settle down," Daddy said. He got up and opened the kitchen drawer. Looking for the can opener.

I knew that we were trying our best to hold out until that Sunday afternoon bucket of chicken. Me? I'd've given the stars for just one of Burma's drumsticks right then and there.

# Twelve

Sometimes when I came in from school, I noticed that Grenna had forgotten to change out of her nightgown. Or to brush her silver cloud of hair. Or to put on her pink lotion. Before the heart attack, Grenna had *always* put that lotion on first thing after washing in the morning—she called it "putting on her face."

Now she was after me about going through her drawers. "I need to get rid of some of this junk," she'd say. Like I didn't have weeds to pull with Daddy or my science chapter to read for Mr. Farkle's class. To top it off, when I'd make a move to go through some stuff, she'd stop me: "No, not today, I'm not quite up to it."

Grenna wasn't the only one busy going wonky. I'd begun, at the oddest moments, wondering things I'd never given a second thought before. Like walking into the school cafeteria one Thursday, I'd found myself thinking about what Mama's favorite food might have been. Near the end of September, when I woke up suddenly, I'd wished to the moon that I could, just once, hear the sound of her laugh.

In my room, I heard the distant rumble of a train. One of those crazy thoughts popped into my head again, and I found myself wondering if Mama, wherever she was, could hear the train, too. If she could see me and my red hair and freckles, or our tiny yellow house.

I bounded down the stairs, popped in to say a quick hello to Grenna, grabbed my notebook from the counter, and headed out the front door.

My destination was the woods. I wasn't sure if I'd make it by Maranatha, though. I was on assignment today, an English assignment, to be specific. If there was ever a time to be specific, it was for Mrs. Rulanger, my English teacher.

When Mrs. Rulanger spoke, her voice sounded so deep and rich that the word *resounding* came to mind. Her brown skin seemed to glow under the fluorescent lights, and when she walked close to my desk, I could make out little constellations of dots on each of her cheeks that I supposed were tiny moles. The few times Mrs. Rulanger had deigned to peer at me over her half-glasses, I was certain she could see straight down to the center of my soul.

That day in English class, Mrs. Rulanger had given us each a blank sheet of paper and told us to fold it and put it in our back pockets. She then told us our assignment: Find something that *inspires* you and write about it.

"What floats your boat?" she'd asked. "What dings your hum? What yings your yang?"

Jim McClendon asked, "What if I don't have a back pocket?"

Mrs. Rulanger lowered her half-glasses. "Get a fanny pack!"

"And, kids," she said before she turned us loose into the halls of Jubilee Junior High, "remember *the rules*!"

If there was one thing we knew in Mrs. Rulanger's English class, it was *the rules*!

Rule number one for writing composition: "Make it interesting!"

Rule number two was really more of a demand: "Use specific examples!" To reinforce this rule, she would walk around the room slapping a ruler onto various desks and calling out her demand with one word: "Specificity!"

"Be creative! Be correct!" She had repeated this mantra since the first day of school.

I'd pulled out the paper during lunch to write something. At first, I tried thinking about Mr. Farkle's science class and the periodic table of elements. But then Benjamin's melted chocolate eyes popped into my brain. I couldn't write about a boy's eyes, though, so I put the paper back into my pocket.

Our school lunch, an unidentifiable piece of fried, oddly green meat, definitely didn't inspire me either.

Hard as I tried, I just couldn't make Laverne's and Meg's ongoing debate about the uses and misuses of fingernail polish interesting. I thought fingernail polish was good for nothing but stopping the runs in panty hose. Of course, I thought that hose were really good for nothing but stuffing scarecrows.

Meg agreed with me about polish on the fingernails. She didn't like the "yellowing" effect, but she did like to polish her toenails. "They look better in flip-flops that way," she said. Laverne, on the other hand, was a true-blue polish supporter—well, more like true pink or true red, depending on the day.

When we had filed out for the buses at the end of the day, I spotted Colette Violetti sashaying down the hall with her usual entourage of boys—including Benjamin Hartwell. I decided then and there that my "inspiration" was not to be found in the halls of Jubilee Junior High.

So, as I reached the woods, I reveled in how good it felt to be outside.

The brisk air washed over my face and seemed to awaken something in me that had been sleeping all summer.

After picking my way through a maze of branches and briars, I turned my feet toward a fern-lined stream and followed it to the creek.

By the time I arrived at the cedars, the sun was already lowering in the west. I hoped something would "ying my yang" soon, because I wanted to make it back before dark. Although I loved cedar trees, I also thought they were a little spooky. Legend has it that cedar trees are haunted. Some say they're filled with the spirits of the Cherokee who used to live in these foothills, others say they hold the souls of soldiers from the Civil War. As I looked at them in the dimming day, they sure did seem to be straining more than shade out of the evening air.

I held still and looked at the tree, but I didn't feel inspired. So I just listened to the quiet that's not really quiet in the woods: the flowing trickle of water over rocks in the creek, a sudden rustle of leaves that sounds so loud you think it must be a deer but it turns out to be only a brown thrasher scratching in the leaves. I also heard the rough-edged purr of a distant crow and the audacious buzz of a fly orbiting my head. Before I knew it, my senses were all caught up in what I'd come for—the cedar. The first thing that settled into me after the sounds was the smell of it.

I closed my eyes and concentrated on the smell.

I took out my piece of paper and started to write:

**Cedar**
*The cedar tree smells like the first crisp bite of spearmint
    chewing gum,
refreshing, yet almost like medicine in its bitter.*

*This tree is surely as ancient as Ecclesiastes—
that's a book in the Old Testament that I haven't read
    much of,
but it sounds like cedar smells.*

*The scent of cedar holds a perpetual hush,
whispering, "Hush-hush-still-stay."*

*And then the cedar says, "Rush-rush-be-on-your-way,*
*for I have seen children of earth come and go*
*and soldiers live and die,*
*and I hold them all softly in my green-black shade."*

*And so I will leave the cedar*
*to return to its refrain*
*and to remain*
*the green a-men of the forest.*

I shoved the paper deep in my pocket. It was only when I was about halfway home that I realized what I'd written was a poem.

On Saturday, I led Spunky out of the barn and into the pasture, and shoveled out her stall. As I was washing my hands at the spigot, I heard the crunch of Comet's wheels on gravel. Daddy called to Kevin to open the barn door. Then Daddy eased the back of Comet inside the barn. That meant it was time to begin picking seeds.

First, Daddy split open several watermelons we had kept from the summer's crop to harvest the seeds for future planting. The flesh of the fruit was surprisingly red under the blue sky. He handed us each a chunk, and we ate it. The melon was ripe, almost too ripe, and as sweet as candy. I tried to suck the extra juice out of my piece, but it was already dribbling from my chin and trailing down my arm.

After that we took to picking seeds out of the watermelons. When we'd gathered a slew of the slimy, flat, black teardrops, we carried them to the tubs that Daddy was filling with water. Then Daddy took a mesh net and rinsed the seeds again and again until they were free of sugar. If we didn't clean them good, then the ants would be after them or they'd mildew and mold. When they were rinsed, I'd climb up into the loft to lay them out on the drying tables.

It went on and on like that, over and over, hour after hour. That's how seeding is: fun at first, boring for a while, and then you pick so many seeds that you think your fingernails will fall out.

Daddy turned on Comet's radio and let the twangy music croon up to the rafter where the barn owls were snoozing. After a while, we stopped to stretch our backs, and Daddy snapped off the radio. "Don't want to run all the juice out of Comet," he said.

But I knew better. Daddy's usually not one to talk much, but I'd been picking seeds long enough to know that if there's one thing to get some words out of him, it's a seed-picking day.

We ate another chunk of melon to tide us over till suppertime, and when we began picking at the next batch, Daddy started talking.

"Now," he said, "if we had to start over again from scratch, and you could have one thing to start with, what would you choose?"

"What do you mean by 'from scratch'?" Kevin asked.

"Well, like if a lunatic took to setting off one of them bombs," Daddy said.

"Ummm, clean water?" I ventured. I remembered that my fourth-grade science teacher had asked us a question like this once, but I couldn't remember the answer. It might've been a mirror—or maybe that was if you were stranded on a desert island.

"Comic books!" Kevin yelled. "Definitely comic books."

I rolled my eyes at my brother. No wonder Daddy didn't take the trouble to talk much.

"Well, comic books might take your mind off your troubles for a little while, but they wouldn't go far when your stomach started rumbling," Daddy said. "Water's a good thing, but we'd just have to hope the Lord would provide that with the rain—go to the nearest creek or put out some buckets or barrels, and then you'd be set. No, what I have in mind is *seeds*."

"Seeds?" I asked.

"Yes," Daddy said. "Seeds. And I mean seeds from real food, not those crazy, fandangled hybrid types I've heard tell of on the news. See here, in this seed is not just one watermelon but the seeds of future watermelons as well. So, if you look down the line long enough, this very seed could produce the watermelon that feeds your great-grandkids."

I looked at the little black seed—it wasn't even as big as my pinkie fingernail. I was finding it hard to believe it could be that important.

"Of course, you've also got to have the land and the know-how to plant them," Daddy said. "That's what you've learned here on this farm. What I've tried to teach you. Not only for chores' sake but things about how to survive."

We were quiet after that as we worked, letting Daddy's words sink in good.

When it was almost dusk and I was bone-tired and my belly was begging for something more solid than watermelon, I climbed back down the loft ladder for the nine millionth time and Daddy said, "Well, I reckon that's about enough. I'll bet Grenna's got some of them frozen dinners on the table by now."

As we stepped up on the front porch, I glanced back at the barn, glad for the hard work now and the tiny black treasures that we'd gathered and stored for the spring.

# Thirteen

The next Thursday afternoon after homework and chatting with Grenna and chores with Daddy, I set out for the Point. Meg and Laverne and I were meeting up again to mull over the week. It was Meg's weekend to go to her dad's in Atlanta, so I knew we wouldn't be making any weekend plans.

Walking down the driveway, I spotted Kevin at the wheel of Grandpap's old broken-down Ford at the edge of the field. I picked my way across the brown tangle of old watermelon vines, making my way over to him.

The hole we'd dug during summer was still there. We hadn't made it to China, but it was pretty deep.

Kevin cranked the window down in the truck and leaned out.

"Where ya headed?" I asked.

He smiled but then looked up into the distance.

"Do you ever wish we could go back?" he asked.

I peered at him. "Back where?"

He shrugged his shoulders. "I don't know. Back to when we were digging this hole . . . back before Grenna got sick."

So much had changed in only a few months. Meals were now fiascoes, and Grenna was sleeping more and more, even during the day. *Irreparable.* That was the word the doctors had used for Grenna's heart. It wasn't like she'd be in a lot of pain, they said, but as the blood stopped flowing good, she'd start to slow down. Some of the doctors wanted her to stay in a hospital hooked up to machines, but Grenna wouldn't hear of it. "That's no life for me," she said. I looked at Grandpap's pickup truck. I remembered the day he'd announced that she couldn't be fixed anymore. I simply couldn't accept the fact that Grenna was good for nothing but roosting and rusting in the shade.

"Yeah, Kevin," I said, looking back at him steering the truck to some imaginary destination, "I wish we could go back."

At the Point, I stood on the grassy mound and looked out over the valley of woods and meadows and thought about how nothing ever seemed to change in Jubilee.

Except the things I didn't want to. Like Grenna getting sick.

Earlier that day, Mr. Farkle had announced there was too much goofing off in class and he'd assigned us new project partners. Now my partner was Benjamin Hartwell. Meg was stuck with Jim McClendon, and Laverne with Rodney Carver. That change couldn't have been worse.

I scanned the creek below me and followed the tracks that disappeared into the trees. The chant of a mourning dove in the air seemed to me to say "Same . . . same . . . same-same." Yes, everything else was the same ol', same ol'.

In fact, the seasons took forever to change in Jubilee. Here it was October, and it didn't even seem like autumn. No matter which direction I turned, there wasn't so much as a breeze to lift my red hair. The sky was blue. And the trees in every direction were still mostly green, with only the star-shaped leaves of the sweet gums fading to yellow and the dogwoods beginning to tinge purple and red.

Suddenly I heard a rustle behind me and looked back to see Benjamin Hartwell. He stood for a moment and searched the horizon with his dark brown eyes as we heard the first blasting *hoot* of the approaching train. This time it was coming *from* Jubilee. I was glad it was coming; it meant I didn't have to say anything to my new project partner.

The train blasted again and again, and I tried to ignore the call in it this time, especially since Benjamin was there, but the sound still beckoned me.

When the train nosed its way out of the trees, I saw that it was a shiny aluminum-looking passenger train with red, white, and blue stripes painted down its side. I looked at the rows of windows slowly blurring by and tried to make out the faces looking back at me.

I wondered where the faces were going. Where they were coming from. I wondered what they thought of the red-haired girl and brown-eyed boy they saw on the grassy mound. If they thought life was simpler in the little town of Jubilee that they were passing through. Or if they thought peace reigned underneath the rooftops of Sunny Brooke Acres subdivision. I wondered if they'd be surprised to find there was bickering here just like where they were from, and families split up by divorce and disease.

As the train started to wind away, I heard a shuffling in the grass behind me, and I was almost afraid to turn around. Afraid that Benjamin would be able to tell I was hearing things in train whistles, or even that he'd somehow heard it, too. But I need not have worried, because when I turned around, the only thing I saw was Benjamin Hartwell scooting and hopping around like he had firecrackers in his sneakers.

*"Shee-bop, be-loo-bop, waaa-ma-loy."*

To top it off, he was muttering some strange gibberish in the midst of all the leaping.

*"Rinky-tinky, waaa-za-zoo."*

"What in tarnation?" I asked when the last echoes of the train had faded and Benjamin, blessedly, stopped his high jinks.

"Oh, just getting into the rhythm," he said, like he hadn't done a thing.

*What a weirdo,* I thought.

He was talking again. "You know, like—*jazz*—the sound

wrapped up in the silver snake, the rhythms of steel on steel, wheel on track, squeal of brake, and shout of horn." He did another two-step kick and then started making his way down the slope.

He stopped at the foot of the mound, dug in his pocket, and pulled out something that looked like a compass and what looked to be a blue jay feather. "They say Gershwin wrote *Rhapsody in Blue* by listening to the sound of a train," he called back as I heard a burst of giggles behind me.

I turned to see Meg and Laverne arriving.

"Hey," they called to me. "Did we miss anything?"

"Yeah, you *missed it*, all right," I said, laughing and thinking of Benjamin Hartwell.

The girls sat down, but when I looked back toward the valley, Benjamin was gone.

In that instant I heard a whistling cry rise from the far woods, and then, a half a wink later, I saw a hawk lift out of the branches and spiral up into the blue sky.

The next Tuesday, Laverne passed a note to me after science class. I shoved it into my pocket. I gave her a note, too, that said I needed her to deliver the Pseudonymphs' yellow name book to me the next day. She and Meg had been studying up for the fall name change, but I hadn't had a chance. Maranatha's seeds could decide to twirl any time now.

I read Laverne's note in gym class, waiting for the coach to take roll.

*Dear Millicent,*

*It's worse than I thought. Rodney wants to do our science project on peanuts. Something about if it takes them longer to mold in the shell or out. I'm completely disgusted.*

*By the way, have you and Benjamin come up with a project yet?*

*Other news: a pair of crows have started roosting in the pine tree in our front yard. Isn't that gross? Every morning I wake up to hear them squawking away— almost as loud as my parents.*

*Later, Camilla*

I refolded the note.

After English class, Meg passed me a note. I shoved it in my other pocket. Once Meg and Laverne and the Sunny Brooke crowd filed off the bus that day, I read it.

*Dear Millicent,*

*It's not as bad as I thought. Jim McClendon thinks that a science project on "The Flop Effect" is a great idea! He's even agreed to wear flip-flops for the rest of the semester. I'm going over to his house this afternoon for the preliminary measurements.*

*By the way, I found out where your lab partner was last Friday. He'd skipped school to supposedly track a hawk to its nest. Something to do with a Cherokee rit-*

*ual. I'll bet Farkle and his parents didn't fall for that one! He'll probably be on restrictions for six months!*

*I had a good weekend with my dad—we went to a Braves game.*

*Soon, Jeanette*

I finished refolding the note just as the bus pulled up to our slightly sagging mailbox, and I bounded down the two stairs.

While I walked back up the driveway, I thought about how notes are kind of like quarters—it's always nice to know you've got some in your pockets.

"The Flop Effect," Meg announced at the Point the next day after school. She promptly slipped off her flip-flops and began staring intently at her toes.

"The Flop Effect?" Laverne asked as she crisscrossed her legs on the grass.

"Yeah. See the space between my big toe and pointer? As Mr. Farkle would say, 'it's my hypothesis' that flip-flops are kind of like backward braces for feet—wearing them all the time is creating a space."

"Hey, you should watch out for that," Laverne said. "I read once that if we didn't have toes, we couldn't walk."

I looked at Meg's feet. "Seems funny those little nubbins could be so important," I said, wondering why in the world Jim McClendon had agreed to wear flip-flops for the rest of the semester to test the hypothesis.

Meg shrugged. "Anyway, Camilla," she said, looking

around to make sure that no one was spying on us. "Did you notice that Rodney Carver was staring at you during science class today?"

Laverne turned as red as the inside of a Rattlesnake watermelon. "He *was* not, Jeanette."

Meg slipped her flip-flops back on. "Was, too," she insisted.

"You know what we need to do?" I said, picking at some grass. "Come up with something to cure Mr. Farkle's class of Rodney Carver, Jim McClendon, and Benjamin Hartwell."

Laverne and Meg laughed.

"What about you, Camilla?" I asked. "Still thinking of the peanut mold project with Rodney Carver?"

Laverne got up, slipped off her glasses, and walked to the edge of the Point. She was quiet for a minute and then said, "Actually, the only thing I'm interested in is something to cure parents of the *divorce* disease."

Meg and I looked at each other.

We went over, each put an arm around Laverne, and led her back to the hump so we could sit down again.

"Okay, Cam," I said. "What's going on?"

She told us her parents had always argued—it was par for the course. But now it was becoming a nightly thing. Last night, she'd heard her dad use the D word during an argument.

"It's been getting worse for a while, though," she said. "Really since we moved into the new house in Sunny Brooke. It's like they thought a bigger, better house would make them happy, but it really stressed them out more."

Meg and I didn't know what to say.

Laverne sniffed, slipped her glasses back on, and looked at us. She only nodded, but we knew it was enough for now.

My stomach rumbled loudly. School lunch had definitely worn off. I hopped up, and we headed down the grassy mound to the trail.

When the last kernel of popcorn was eaten, we walked into the living room. Daddy got up and snapped off the TV.

"March Anne," he said, heading to the door, "I'm going to check on the pumpkins. Them squash beetles are about to eat up all the young Tricky Jacks this year."

*Squash beetles?*

I looked at Meg and Laverne and yelled, "*That's it!* The topic for my science project!"

My mind was already sprinting to the Feed 'n' Seed and to what combinations of poisons or traps I'd buy to eradicate the pesty buggers as we rushed into Grenna's room. We found her sitting in the rocking chair and looking out the window. I blurted out my plan to declare war on squash beetles.

"Squash beetles?" she said, her eyes brightening. "We had a problem with those years ago. They'll eat up young pumpkins faster than you can say lickety-split. Now, I have that recipe somewhere. June Cobb gave it to me in Sunday school class—she always had the greenest thumb I ever knew of!"

Recipe? June Cobb? Sunday school? What in tarnation was Grenna talking about? *Please, Lord, don't let Grenna start up with the wonky talk in front of Meg and Laverne,* I prayed.

But Grenna was already scooting her metal elephant over to the dresser, and Laverne was talking to her like nothing was weird about a recipe for squash beetles.

"Yes, ma'am," Laverne was saying, "my mom sprays a garlic-and-mint mix on the roses—it does the trick every time."

Garlic? Mint? Maybe Laverne was going wonkers, too.

Grenna was now opening her drawers stuffed with scarves and ancient, empty bottles. *Why won't she get rid of those things?* Meg, oblivious, was chiming in.

"Did you ever try liquid dish soap mixed with seltzer water?" she asked. "My mom swears by it."

I realized then and there that they were one big happy family of wonkies.

With every dresser drawer open, the eucalyptus rub smell from all the empty tubs Grenna'd saved was so strong it was making my eyes sting. I looked over at Meg and Laverne to see how they could stand it. But they were still jabbering away.

"No," Grenna said, rummaging through a tangle of pink and purple scarves. "I think this one had rubbing alcohol in it, maybe some onion, and a dollop of turpentine."

I couldn't take it anymore. "What in tarnation are y'all talking about?"

"The recipe for squash beetle repellent," Grenna told me flatly.

"You mean . . . ?" I began weakly.

"Yeah," Laverne replied. "You can make up your own concoction to chase away the buggers."

"One that won't kill the honeybees and ladybugs," added Meg.

"Aha," I murmured. I hadn't thought of concocting my own repellent, but it was a great idea.

Grenna was fishing white jewelry boxes out of her sea of silky aqua and azure neckerchiefs. Inside each tiny box was a square cloud of cotton.

"Well, I know one thing," I said. "If you can find a recipe for squash beetle repellent in all that, you *will* deserve the Nobel Prize!"

Laverne and Meg chuckled, but Grenna had just fished a small book out of a bright red scarf.

"Well, will you look at that?" she said as she held up an old schoolbook—the Haliburton *Second Reader.*

"What? Is the recipe in there?" I asked.

"Oh, no," Grenna said. "I'd forgotten I had this." She opened the book, and we found pressed flowers were hidden in between the yellowed pages. A few violets. A four-leaf clover. And a dandelion.

"I didn't know people pressed *dandelions*," I said. "Aren't they weeds?"

"Well, no. Not to everyone," Grenna said with a distant look in her eyes. "Meg, you belong to the Finchers, right—the *Cherokee* Finchers?"

"Yes, ma'am," she answered.

"Well, I knew your great-grandmother. I used to pass her farm on the way into town. And in the early spring she'd keep her yard full of dandelions. They just bloomed out as pretty as you please, like a sea of tiny yellow suns. No, you didn't think about weeds if you saw a sight as pretty as that. It's only when people started planting grass and such that dandelions became weeds."

Meg looked into the shadowy corner of the drawer as if she was half-proud, half-embarrassed to learn this about her ancestor.

"It's a shame your great-grandma has gone on," Grenna continued, looking at Meg. "She could have told us a thing or two about how to take care of squash beetles."

"All this rummaging has wore me plumb out," Grenna said after we'd gone through two more drawers of ancient girdles and brassieres that looked big enough to hold Moon 'n' Stars watermelons.

"Me, too," Meg said, redoing her ponytail in Grenna's dresser mirror.

"Me, tutu," Laverne agreed, yawning hugely.

"What about the recipe?" I asked.

"You might try the hall closet," Grenna said, turning back her quilt.

The hall closet was a place we Tanners didn't go into much—not the younger generation, anyway. It served as a kind of attic, and I knew there were Christmas decorations in there, but I didn't know what else.

"What's in these boxes?" Meg asked when I opened the door.

"I don't know," I admitted. "Probably a boatload of junk."

"Or a boatload of spiders," Laverne said, making sure her glasses were on properly to spot any of the scurrying creatures.

"Well, squash beetles await," I announced, pulling the first box toward me and opening it.

That afternoon we found lots of stuff we weren't looking for.

A broken bow and a leather quiver of arrows. "Probably my grandpap's," I told the girls.

A box of knitting needles and balls of different-colored yarn. "Probably Grenna's," I said.

An ancient, moth-eaten white flannel nightgown that we promptly threw out.

A sewing machine that had definitely been Grenna's. I could still remember when she sewed my Sunday go-to-preaching dresses.

Some bottles of putrefied whiskey, which we also threw out. "*Definitely* Grandpap's." Grenna had told me how Grandpap's whiskey had poisoned their "sweetest little place." He took to drinking there when one of his dark moods came on, and Grenna said she'd never been back.

A rectangular can of she-lack from Grenna's arts-and-crafts days.

Just then the screen door swung open and Kevin walked in. He grabbed an old trench coat from the closet and started singing into an invisible microphone, while dancing like Fred Astaire.

We laughed, and Kevin pulled out the contents of the coat pockets. In his right hand, he held five mothballs that looked like tiny white eggs, and in his left hand, he held an index card that turned out to be—you guessed it—June Cobb's squash beetle recipe!

We read the recipe aloud and found Grenna'd been right about the rubbing alcohol and turpentine.

Daddy put down his newspaper in the living room and shook his head. "You girls be careful concocting that stuff," he said. "We don't want to be setting off no bombs around here!"

"What in tarnation?" I exclaimed, wincing at the stronger-than-ever eucalyptus rub scent in the air when I walked in from school on Friday. Meg and Laverne were coming over later to spend the night and help launch the squash beetle project the next day.

I followed the smell into Grenna's room. Once again, her dresser drawers were open and stuff was cluttered onto every horizontal surface. Empty bottles and jars of all shapes and sizes stood on the dresser. Colorful scarves and empty jewelry boxes were clumped together on the bedside table. Stacks of old seed catalogs sat on the rocking chair. And what looked to be a mountain of old panty hose were piled up on the bed.

"I've finally decided to go through this junk, March Anne," Grenna told me.

"Hallelujah!" I yelled.

"Well, don't just stand there gaping like an old scarecrow," she said. "Come hold this trash bag open for me."

"Yes, ma'am," I said, imagining how good it would feel to scrape all the bottles off the dresser in one fell swoop.

When I picked up an old jar and started to put it in the bag, Grenna stopped me.

"Whoa, there, March Anne—not that one," she said, examining it closely. "Yes, still perfectly good," she announced. "We might could use that for something." I really did gape when she put it back in her drawer. What in the world would we ever use an empty eucalyptus rub tub for?

As the bottles and jars went back in the drawer, I brought up the subject that I'd come to mull over with her.

"Grenna," I said. "Don't you think that there's a lot in a name?"

"What do you mean?" she asked, finally plopping two cracked plastic medicine bottles into the trash bag.

"I mean like the way a name sounds," I went on, struggling to find the words for what I was getting at. "Or maybe even in what it means. Take the name Benjamin Hartwell, for instance. Isn't that a nice sounding name?"

"Oh, yes," she said. "That's a good name. Benjamin is a biblical name, just like your grandpap's name, Samuel."

"What about the Hartwell part?"

"I like that, too. It reminds me of a lake my papa took us to to go swimming once when we were little. I remember thinking then that the 'Hart'—that's another name for a deer—could live 'well' by all that beautiful water."

"Yeah," I agreed. "I was thinking something like that, too."

Grenna opened an ancient medicine bottle, and I caught a whiff of a putrid smell. She put it back in the drawer.

"Grenna, that medicine is prehistoric," I said. "You've got to throw that away!"

"No, dear, we can't throw medicine away. We spent good money on it. Who knows, it might be good for something."

"Yeah, for killing squash beetles," I said. Still, she put the petrified medicine back in the drawer and closed it. Daddy had explained to me once that folks who lived through the Great Depression had a hard time parting with things, but this was ridiculous.

"You know what your name would've been if you'd been a boy, don't you?" she asked, refolding an orange neckerchief and placing it back in the drawer.

"Kevin?" I ventured.

"Oh, no. Your mama and daddy had it picked out. You were going to be McGuirty, for my maiden name; March, for your grandpap's surname; and, of course, Tanner."

"McGuirty March Tanner?" I repeated in disbelief. I'd thought March Anne was bad. "What boy can go through life with a name like McGuirty March?"

"Oh," Grenna said, laughing, "they'd have probably taken to calling you Mac or Archy or something."

That didn't console me much. McGuirty was Kevin's middle name, not his first. "How'd Kevin get off the McGuirty hook?"

"Oh, I don't know," she said. "I guess they didn't like it as much for a first name without the March."

I reminded myself to tell Kevin that he should be eternally grateful I was born before him.

"Well, the white gown is not here," Grenna said, sighing and picking up the last scarf. "I know it's got to be around here somewhere, and I need it so badly. You know your mama sewed it for me, and it was just the right weight to keep me warm. I do declare that the dampness in the air today is going right through me."

*There goes Grenna with the wonky talk again,* I thought, looking out the window at the warm day and the clear, blue sky of a Georgia autumn. It was true that we'd had some cooler weather, but it was hot enough today to wear shorts. I remembered the moth-eaten gown we'd found in the hall closet, but somehow I didn't have the heart to tell her we'd trashed it. I'd have to talk to Daddy about how to make it up to her.

After Grenna and I put a stack of old catalogs back in the bottom dresser drawer, I looked in the trash bag. It contained two cracked medicine bottles, one ripped scarf, three pairs of old panty hose, and a catalog receipt. That was it.

"Old medicine bottles, ancient glue, out-of-date seed catalogs," I said, surveying the last drawer before I closed it. "Grenna, why are you keeping this junk?"

Grenna smiled and touched her cloud of silver hair. "You know, March Anne, one day it might be good for something."

"For *what*?"

"Decoupage," she said, flatly.

I snorted.

Then Grenna laughed.

And I laughed with her.

# Fourteen

*I*s Benjamin here yet?" Meg asked, bounding down the creakity stairs the next morning.

"Nah," I said, surveying the kitchen counter. Everything was here: turpentine, rubbing alcohol, liquid dish soap, whiskey, garlic, onions, and pepper sauce. If this didn't run off those squash beetles, nothing would!

Laverne picked a Granny Smith apple out of a bowl on the counter. "What if he doesn't show?"

I shrugged. "Then I'll do the project myself. Which is probably what I'll end up doing anyway."

"What did he think of the idea—I mean the squash beetles and all?" Meg asked.

"I don't know. I told him in Mr. Farkle's class that it's what we were doing."

Laverne looked shocked. "You *told* him?"

We jerked our heads toward the door when we heard a loud knock.

"Yep," I said, glancing back at them as I went to let Benjamin in.

About an hour later we were armed with squirt bottles filled with our lethal concoctions. We'd taken June Cobb's recipe and improvised a bit. I'd added more turpentine to mine. Benjamin had added more whiskey, Meg more liquid soap, and Laverne more pepper sauce. Out in the front field of pumpkins, we each staked out our patches with labels.

"Let the battle begin!" I declared.

Soon thereafter Laverne sneezed violently enough to knock her glasses off her nose.

I looked up at her. "Bless you," I said.

Benjamin started guffawing with glee. "It's working!" he hollered. We looked over and saw a troop of the tiny, black-and-red-striped bugs retreating from the patch of Tricky Jack pumpkins. Laverne sneezed again.

"What're you trying to do, Laverne?" I asked. "Wake up every attic bat from here to Chattanooga?"

"I don't know, but I think—*ah-chooo*—I'm allergic—*ah-ahhh*—to pepper—*choooooooo*—spray," she said.

"Let's hope the squash beetles are allergic, too," Meg said, taking a moment to stretch her back and pull her ponytail tight.

Benjamin laughed at the joke, and I offered to trade patches and squirt bottles with Laverne; the sneezes finally subsided into sniffles.

When we had moved on to another patch of pumpkins and our backs were starting to ache, Benjamin spoke into the silence. "Y'all hear the latest about ol' Crabapple Crutcher?" he asked.

"Nah," we said.

He went on to tell us about how a flock of grackles had been roosting in the oak at Crabapple's shack. One day, he'd seen Crabapple up on a ladder poking her head in among the cackling grackles.

"As I turned to go," he concluded, "I noticed something bright as a knife blade sticking up from the top of the oak. I guess it was an old antenna or a lightning rod or something."

"Maybe Crabapple's got herself a new TV," Meg said.

Laverne chuckled. "Or maybe she's really a spy and is signaling Jubilee's governmental secrets to national enemies."

"It's hard to say," Benjamin said, peering off into the distance. "It's really hard to say."

After we were done, we washed our hands at the barn spigot and plopped down on the front porch, exhausted.

Benjamin kept hanging around like he thought I'd invite him to supper or something, but I wasn't letting on that we didn't eat anything but frozen dinners or mishmash pie since Grenna's heart attack.

Finally, he stood up and looked at me with his melted-chocolate eyes. "Well, see you at school," he said, and headed down the driveway.

"See you," I called.

When he was out of sight, Laverne said, "Did you get a load of all that hogwash he was feeding us?"

"Yeah," Meg agreed. "Like Crabapple could really climb a ladder at her age. She's ancient!"

I didn't say anything. Secretly, though, I thought that he might've been telling the truth. He had a look of honesty about him. Especially in the eyes.

The next afternoon, after preaching at Mars Hill Baptist and a Burma Bucket, the clouds settled over Jubilee.

It was a hard rain. Steady. The type of rain that would knock the leaves off the trees before they had a chance to color up good.

I put on my yellow slicker and darted from the house to the red barn. I wanted to be out in the day, to be a part of it. For, despite the fact that rain was sorry autumn weather, I did love rainy days. Especially rainy days spent under the tin roof of a barn.

I slipped off my soaked slicker, hung it on a peg, and began my rounds. The gray light streamed through the windows, and although it was rather hard to see at first, I chose not to turn on the lantern. The light matched the day—and the smell of hay that filled the barn seemed to cling and linger even stronger in the dim light.

After I cleaned out Spunky's stall, I turned my attention to the high rafter where the white barn owls were perched. Oddly enough, they weren't sound asleep. When I first glimpsed up, I'd caught Wynken swiveling his head around. Then he'd held it still, as if he didn't want to admit that he'd been spying on me. Blynken held his head at a half turn, but I could see that his left eye was open. And Nod, he was wide awake and glaring at me with both brown eyes as if he were blaming me for the commotion the rain was making on the tin roof.

I reached for the rough wooden rung of the ladder and climbed up to the hayloft. At the top, I finally spied a furry mound within the scattered straw. I walked over, scratched Dorcas behind her left ear, and listened to her add her nuzzly, buzzing purr to the steady rhythm of the rain. Dorcas's purr sounded like the feeling the rain gave me—warm inside and content with nothing more than a tin roof and the smell of hay.

*Dorcas*—now there's another name for you. That's the name Grenna gave to the bedraggled kitten who'd turned up one day in the middle of the watermelon patch years ago. The baby cat had been through something terrible. She had a torn ear, a broken tail, and shredded fur. That's why Grenna had named her after the girl in the Bible who Peter the Apostle brought back to life. Like the biblical Dorcas, our kitten had cheated death and gained a second chance. Since then, our cat has enjoyed a good life, squabbling with the owls over the mice and other varmints that dare to show themselves in the Tanner barn.

I suddenly remembered another rainy afternoon. I couldn't have been much more than a toddler, and someone had carved a dollhouse out of a watermelon rind for me. I had played with it on that rainy afternoon right here in the barn. The watermelon rind had a little door and windows, and I could lift off the top to put in my dolls. Who had made it for me? Daddy? Grandpap?

The watermelon-rind dollhouse reminded me of Grenna's story of the place where she and Grandpap had lived when they were first married. Whenever I'd asked Grenna about it over the years, she'd always just said that the little place had gone sour with Grandpap's liquor and wasn't fit to visit. Then she'd get that far-off look like she was reading something in the sky.

A huge thunderclap startled me from my thoughts and sent me back to the present in the hayloft. I curled up in the straw next to Dorcas. Yes, she had the right idea. I listened to the rain rumbling over the tin roof like a train on its tracks. Somehow, there seemed to be a lullaby in its loudness. With Dorcas snuggled close to my chest, I settled in for an afternoon nap.

In the dream that came to me, I was a child in the rain. My red hair was bound up in pink ribbons, and I was dancing and twirling. I was dripping wet. It must've been summer because the rain was warm and something smelled sweet within it. My face was tilted up, and I was chanting to the clouds. But I couldn't make out the words of my chant.

I saw Grenna standing on the porch beckoning to me with her hand like a traffic cop. "Come in out of the rain, March Anne. Come in out of the rain, child," she was hollering.

Instead of obeying, I ran farther out into the field. Something—*was it the rain?*—was calling me, "Come . . . come . . .

Find . . . find . . ." I had to follow the voice that was calling me toward the woods. I wanted to keep running and for the rain to keep falling on my chubby cheeks and tickling my stuck-out tongue.

I was laughing as I ran in my dream, chasing something I couldn't define. It was out there, in the rain. And I knew if I just kept running, and the rain kept falling, I would be able to find it.

When I woke up, I wondered what the dream meant. I knew, somehow, that it was connected to the call. The dream was somehow another clue to where I was supposed to go, what I was supposed to find.

That Tuesday I walked to Maranatha and saw her seeds swirling in the air like so many tiny helicopters. I told Meg and Laverne about it at school the next day during lunch, and we decided to meet just before sunset.

As we made our way across the fallow field, I saw that most of the clover had begun to shrivel in the October air. The tips of the forest trees were just piercing the yolk of the lowering sun. A breeze lifted my hair, and I looked at my friends and smiled. I could see that they felt it, too: fall was finally arriving in Jubilee, Georgia.

When we reached Maranatha, the wind picked up, sending a flutter of hundreds of winged seeds into the air. We ran to catch as much of the whirling confetti as we could, thanking Maranatha with our shouts and shrieks of delight.

After we'd each caught a handful of seeds, we fell to the

ground, giggling and out of breath. The tiny seeds and the slanting sunlight caught in our hair, and our cheeks glowed red from the running and reaching as we sat in a circle with our legs crisscrossed. It was time for the fall name exchange.

I cleared my throat and lifted my handful of seeds above my head. "As Maranatha releases her seeds in the autumn wind, we release our own names under this sky: March Anne, once Millicent, will now be Josephina."

Laverne lifted her seeds above her head. "And I, Laverne, once Camilla, shall now be called Raquela."

Meg also lifted her handful of twirlers. "Here I release my old names Meg and Jeanette and claim my new name, Desiree."

The sunset was now a fire in the sky beyond the web of trees, and we stood and threw Maranatha's seeds up into the breeze. As the winged seeds swirled back down toward the ground, our laughter floated up and out through branches and leaves, mingling with the last of the day's golden light.

# Fifteen

As the end of October rolled around, I found myself in a jam—literally. The annual Pumpkin Patch held on our farm was only days away. Daddy had a nice crop of pumpkins, but this year we wouldn't have Grenna's preserves and pies to sell, and I was determined to remedy this.

We'd hoped that Grenna would feel well enough to make some pumpkin goodies at the last minute, but her doctor wouldn't allow it. So, I knew it was up to me.

I took out the pressure cooker and set to making Grenna's famous pumpkin preserves.

*I can do this,* I thought. After all, I knew how to follow the directions for mixing peroxide and baking soda for lava in Mr. Farkle's class. Cooking was just "domesticated science," right?

When I scraped the preserves from the metal cooker into the glass Mason jar, I was encouraged to see that the jelly was the same peachy color as I'd remembered Grenna's preserves being. I couldn't wait for the first taste.

A dollop of jam globbed onto my fingers. When I went to wipe off the beautifully golden concoction, I discovered that it wouldn't budge.

I tried washing my hands. With soap. With warm water. With vinegar. And then with Vaseline. But nothing seemed to work. I must have put something way wrong into the preserves.

I decided it was time for extreme measures. I went to Grenna's room to find her eucalyptus rub. Grenna was always rubbing that gunk on us as kids, so maybe it would unstick my homemade superglue. I found Grenna dozing, as usual, and went over to her dresser.

When I unscrewed the aqua-green lid, memories of Grenna slathering the gel on our chests when we'd had colds came flooding back. I rubbed the eucalyptus gunk on my hands, and, oddly enough, the jam finally budged from my fingers.

I realized that I'd better dispose of my petrified pumpkin preserves before somebody's tongue got stuck to the roof of their mouth—permanently.

When I got back to the kitchen, Daddy already had a spoonful of the jam heading straight toward his mouth.

"No, Daddy. *Don't!*"

Fortunately, he suspended the spoon just in time.


I woke up early on Saturday and remembered with a rush that the Pumpkin Patch was today.

Today.

I jumped out of bed. It was time for action.

When Grenna was still up and running the show, the Pumpkin Patch had been a weeklong fanfare of kindergarten field trips, retired people's tours, and sales, sales, sales of jams, jellies, pies, and pumpkins, pumpkins, pumpkins.

Now it had been boiled down to one measly day.

And, unfortunately, the only thing I'd been able to cook up so far was superglue for jack-o'-lanterns.

I wasn't giving up, however. I knew that Daddy needed this pumpkin sale to help make ends meet on the Tanner farm, and, by golly, I was going to give it my best effort. Kevin was already out with Daddy setting up tables and such around the barn.

Laverne and Meg gathered at my side.

"Raquela, Desiree, this is Grenna's secret recipe for pumpkin pies," I announced, wielding the index card from the recipe box. "That's what the people come for, and that's what we're gonna make sure they get."

"Well, Josephina, what's the to-do about? It shouldn't be that hard," Laverne said as she pulled her curly blond mass of hair into a rubber band.

Meg tied one of Grenna's old aprons around her waist. "Yeah, Josey," she said, "why else would people say 'as easy as pie'?"

An image of my mishmash pie flashed through my mind. I wasn't so convinced.

"Maybe it won't be hard for you gals," I said, "but I am very *challenged* when it comes to recipes. In fact, to be on the safe side, I don't even want to hold it any longer. Desiree, you read. Just tell me what ingredients we need and what to do."

Laverne and I soon set to work scraping the orange, fleshy sides out of pie pumpkins while Meg filled the air with the sweet, warm scents of cinnamon, sugar, and nutmeg.

Then Laverne whipped.

Meg stirred.

And I held the pie crusts as they ladled in the orange pie filling.

"See, Josephina," Meg said as she shoved the last pie in the oven, "easy as pie." I didn't say anything then, but I couldn't help but notice that our foreign-sounding names somehow didn't fit the whole pumpkin motif. In fact, I wasn't sure they fit us at all.

The six pies would take over an hour to bake, so we set about tying orange ribbons to fence posts and grouping together sunflowers in bright, wide-eyed bunches.

As I walked back by the barn, I was glad to see that Kevin had stuffed one of Daddy's shirts with hay and was painting the triangle nose on the T-shirt face of a scarecrow.

"That looks great, Kevin," I said.

"If you think this is cool, check out what Daddy's doing," Kevin said, nodding his head toward the barn.

I walked into the barn and saw Daddy was harnessing up Spunky. But it wasn't any old harness. It was twirled and twisted around with ribbon and colorful chrysanthemums. Then I saw the wagon that was usually parked and forlorn behind the barn. Daddy had decorated it with more ribbon and festive flowers. *Hayrides!* I'd almost forgotten about hayrides.

Maybe the Pumpkin Patch was going to be a success, despite all the changes.

"Wow, it's beautiful," I said. Daddy lifted his head and met my smile with a smile.

As I studied a yellow chrysanthemum, Grenna came to mind. She'd always called the wagon her "carriage," and loved to take rides in it when I was little. I wondered how Grenna was doing today.

I turned back toward the house, and a sharp smell assaulted my nose. Something was burning.

The pies.

By some small miracle, we made a week's worth of sales in one day at the Pumpkin Patch.

The kindergarteners came, but instead of on school field trips, they came with their parents and brothers and sisters.

The retired people came, but instead of arriving together on Wednesday afternoon church group trips, they brought their grandchildren.

People were swarming all over our farm. Some chose the Tallman variety of pumpkin, some the Tricky Jacks, while others opted for the traditional Mammoth Golds or the huge, round Oz pumpkins.

Laverne, Meg, and I worked at a table, taking money for pumpkins and helping children select smaller pumpkins and squashes. My favorite on the children's table were the tiny, fat Baby Boo pumpkins.

On a table behind us sat the burned pumpkin pies—gladly forgotten in the rush.

After Spunky pulled the last hayride through the pumpkin patch, Daddy unharnessed her for a special bath and treat back at the barn. At nightfall, families with smaller children headed home and the older kids started to gather in groups. Laverne made some hot spiced cider while my dad built a little bonfire. I opened a bag of marshmallows, and Kevin and Meg set off to search for roasting twigs.

Finally, everyone gathered around the sparking fire with spiced cider and began roasting marshmallows. Colette Violetti was debating the merits of tall versus fat jack-o'-lanterns with a cluster of her friends. Benjamin Hartwell was sitting next to his cohorts from science class. Many people were unidentifiable as they had put on rubber monster masks and ghost sheets over their heads.

Benjamin was the first to speak into the silence. "Have y'all heard the latest about Ol' Lady Crutcher?" he asked.

"I heard at the library that Mrs. Brumble's cats were found drowned in a bag in Willow Bank Creek last Saturday," Jim McClendon said. "Sounds like the work of Crabapple to me."

In the pause that followed, a log shifted in the fire and sent up a spray of orange sparks into the air. I examined the marshmallow on the end of my twig. Yes, it was roasted to perfection, almost burned on the outside and gooey and warm on the inside.

"My neighbor's dog was poisoned two weeks ago Tuesday," Rodney Carver announced. "I don't know that she did it, but I saw Ol' Crabapple spooking around the subdivision one evening about that same time."

"Me, too," Laverne said, thoughtfully sipping her spiced cider, and the flames danced in her glasses. "I saw her, too. I thought it odd because she was poking around at some milkweed plants."

"Milkweed?" Meg asked, as she pushed three marshmallows onto her stick. "My mom told me that you can eat the leaves of it, but those purple berries are poison."

In the light of the fire, I noticed that Kevin's eyes had grown as big as Baby Boo pumpkins. I also noticed that Colette Violetti kept looking back over her shoulder at the gathering shadows near the edges of the pumpkin patch.

"Interesting," Benjamin said. "That's all very interesting, but it's not the latest."

The fire sparked deep in his melty eyes as he began his tale.

"Well, you'd think if I had the brains of that straw man over there, I'd make for certain sure that I don't run after the hawk in Crabapple's neck of the woods. But the other day, when we got that rain shower, I was looking for the hawk when I heard a thunderclap loud enough to knock me out of my sneakers, and I knew that it'd hit right smack-dab at the Crutcher shack. It was still raining pretty steady, but I knew there wasn't nothing for me to do but go. I had to find out what that lightning had hit.

"When I got to the shack, I heard a howl followed by the

cackling laugh of Ol' Crabapple. I could tell it was coming from the backyard, so I pressed myself up against the shack and peered around the corner. The thing that hit me then was the silence. Then the old lady spat, and I noticed the dark objects scattered across her yard. Crabapple was picking them up and plopping them into a sack and yowling with delight.

"I can be pretty slow sometimes, and it took me a few more seconds to realize that the dark things were the blackbirds. Then I guessed what had happened. The old lady had rigged up a lightning rod in that oak and had French-fried every one of those grackles."

We all looked at him, our mouths hanging open. Forgotten marshmallows dripped and drooped off our twigs, melting away into the flames of the bonfire.

"No way," Laverne finally declared.

Benjamin shrugged. "Go see for yourself," he retorted. "She'll probably leave that ol' lightning rod up there. Just look and see if you spot a blackbird."

Colette Violetti was checking over her shoulder again.

"Wow, what a creepy story," Meg said as she shoved another marshmallow onto her twig in obvious delight.

"Yeah," Colette Violetti said, sounding spooked. "This was fun, but I've got to get goin' home."

"Yeah, time to go," Jim McClendon agreed.

The crowd cleared, and Meg, Laverne, and I started taking down decorations and picking up dropped cider cups until we were foot-weary and bone-tired.

After I pulled down the last of the orange ribbons on the fence posts, I heard a *smack-kerplop* followed by a stream of giggles back near the barn.

I spotted Meg. She had found our burned pumpkin pies and sent one hurling at the straw man. It had smacked him right in the face.

Laverne was laughing and already aiming the next pie.

Another bull's-eye.

By the time we'd thrown another, Kevin and Daddy had joined in the fun. I ran back to the table and grabbed the last pie.

"Wait," a voice said behind me.

I turned to see Benjamin Hartwell standing there with his hands in his pockets.

"I didn't know you were still here," I said.

"Yeah, just helping your brother clean up a little around back," he said. He eyed the pie in my hand. "Didn't you bake those to sell?"

I nodded. "But we burned them, so they're not any good."

"I'll take one," he said. "How much?"

I figured he wanted to take a shot at the scarecrow, too.

"You can have it for free."

"No, I've made me a little money stocking shelves for my dad down at the Feed 'n' Seed. It's about to burn a hole in my pocket," he said. "How much?"

"Well," I replied. "When they're good, they usually go for five dollars."

Benjamin handed me a five.

I shrugged and handed him the pie, waiting for him to throw his best shot at the straw man.

But he kept ahold of the pie and stood there grinning like he'd just won a blue ribbon at the Jubilee Watermelon Festival.

Weird.

# Sixteen

On Halloween night, Laverne and I gathered at Meg's house.

Meg greeted us at the door wearing a pointy witch's hat and black flip-flops decorated with small plastic pumpkins.

I laughed at the getup, but even though we were getting old for trick-or-treating, I still secretly hoped that we'd all put on some old wigs, grab some bags, and hit a few houses. In the meantime, it was fun to be in Sunny Brooke Acres. There were way more houses than out toward our farm, and more houses meant more trick-or-treaters. We loved seeing the little kids dressed up like bunnies and princesses, pirates and superheroes. When we weren't handing out treats, we watched scary movies on TV and munched on candy and popcorn.

When the big rush of kids seemed to be over and we were thinking of turning off the porch light, the doorbell rang. It was three boys dressed in ghoulish rubber masks.

"Aren't y'all a little tall for trick-or-treating?" Laverne asked.

"Yeah," I said, squinting into the eyehole of one of the goblin masks.

The boys stayed put.

"Um, excuse me, but you have to say 'trick or treat,' " said Meg, peering at them from beneath her witch hat.

Still, the boys didn't say a word.

"Well, I guess we better close up shop," I said, reaching for the door to pull it shut.

One of the boys laughed. "All right, trick or treat," he said. Coming through the mask, the words sounded strangely boiled. Yet, even through the muffler, I knew the voice belonged to Benjamin Hartwell.

The boys pulled off their masks. Sure enough, it was Benjamin. Rodney Carver and Jim McClendon were with him.

We gave them candy and chomped on some ourselves.

"Hey," said Benjamin, "we're just about to pay a visit to Ol' Crabapple's shack. Y'all want to come along?"

"No," said Laverne.

"Double no," Meg seconded.

"Ummm," I said, looking at my two best friends, "conference?"

We told the boys to wait as we convened in the living room.

I knew it was a foolish idea, but ever since Benjamin had told the story at the Pumpkin Patch, I'd been curious. Had he been telling the truth? What was that old lady up to back there, anyway?

I tried to convince the girls. "Come on," I whispered. "It's

*Halloween*, after all. We're supposed to do something scary."

"March Anne Tanner, I'm not going in those woods at night," Laverne said flatly.

"She's right, March Anne," Meg agreed. "No way."

"We'll walk around the road," I argued. "No woods. And we'll wear those silly wigs and scarves we wore for the sock hop last year, so if she sees us we'll pretend to be trick-or-treating."


When the six of us turned our feet down the dirt driveway that led to the Crutcher shack, I wondered what I could've been thinking. I mean, I'd been riding past this kudzu jungle of a driveway in Comet for years, but I wasn't so sure it was such a good idea to actually walk down it at night.

Laverne piped up. "Will someone please remind me *why* we are doing this?"

"It's Halloween," I said, trying to reassure myself. "We *have* to do something spooky."

The boys agreed, but I could tell they were as jittery as we were.

As we rounded the final curve, we spotted the shack looming in the darkness. We couldn't see a light in any of the windows.

Meg's flip-flops were slapping steadily into the quiet. "Darn, nobody's home," she said.

"We still have to knock on the door," Benjamin said.

"What if she has a dog?" Jim asked.

"No way," Rodney replied. "She *poisons* dogs, remember?"

Even in the moonlight, I could tell that the shack was more dilapidated than I'd remembered.

When Benjamin opened the broken screen door, it nearly fell right off its hinges.

He lifted his knuckles and rapped three times on the wooden door.

There was no answering sound. Not even a creak.

"Of course she's not here. She's a witch," Laverne said, tossing her blond curls at the moon. "Why would she be home on Halloween?"

Even though I was scared, I wanted to see the tree Benjamin had told us about before we left. I motioned with my head, and he walked with me. We peered around the edge of the shack and caught a glimpse of the oak. Sure enough, a thin silver blade was spiking up into the dark sky.

After that, we hightailed it out of there.

The boys escorted us back to the farm.

By the time we reached the drive, my feet were starting to ache. Even though we hadn't seen Crabapple, we were still spooked from being at her shack.

The wind picked up as we neared the barn, and weblike shadows from the trees danced and swayed across the fields in the moonlight.

Just then I screamed in horror as three white ghosts shrieked out from the barn loft with glowing eyes and lifted into the sky. The others looked up just as a jack-o'-lantern with goblin eyes leaped at us.

Terrified, the six of us took off across the field, tripping over tough, tangled vines. We didn't know where we were going, except that it was *away* from the barn. But when we reached the edge of the woods, an even more frightening apparition greeted us—a witch cackling and spitting. She yowled and heaved a pumpkin toward us.

We hightailed it back to the house. When we finally reached the porch, we were still hollering. In all the rush and muddle, Benjamin kind of crushed into me, and I'm almost positive something wet mashed against my neck. Despite my shock, the only thing I could think about was that smush on my neck.

Could Benjamin have kissed me?

Weird.

And was there a smidgen of my hoping he had?

Double weird.


It was a full two weeks and well into November before Grenna had another "good day." I began calling certain days "crabapples," in honor of ol' Crabapple Crutcher. Some belonged to Grenna: days when she was complaining or chilly or grumpy. On those days, she wanted to go through her drawers and clean things out again, and then she'd snap at me whenever I tried to throw anything away.

Of course, some of the "crabapples" also belonged to me:

days when I was feeling complaining and grumpy because nothing ever changed for the better. Or because I desperately needed a new pair of jeans, but I wouldn't ask Daddy for them because of his furrowed forehead. Or because I had to cook dinner again.

Plus there were the weird things that were happening. Grenna kept talking about a hummingbird I hadn't seen since the summer, I was hearing voices in train whistles and having strange dreams, and witches were stealing Daddy's pumpkins. I was getting very confused and beginning to regret I'd ever wished for change.

Daddy and I had bought Grenna a nice new flowered flannel gown at Belk's department store. It didn't go over well. She said, "No, that won't do. The flannel isn't thick enough."

Grenna was stirring less and less from her bed. And instead of reading or doing crossword puzzles like she used to do, she was sleeping all the time. Then she'd started talking in her sleep. This *definitely* wasn't the change I'd been looking for.

One day she'd been mumbling something about Queen Anne's lace before she woke up suddenly and looked at me. "You know," she said, "your mama's name was Anne."

I looked down, ashamed that I'd forgotten it. To tell the truth, I never really thought about it. Mama was just Mama. A woman with creamy skin and a cloud of red hair in a photograph. A sensation of warmth. A scent of something like vanilla.

I didn't want her to have a name. She might become too real. And then I'd have to miss her.

"There, March Anne, did you see him?" Grenna asked.

I looked out the kitchen window, but I didn't see anything in particular. Not even Nandina and Shout were in view. "No, ma'am, I don't see a thing."

Grenna was spreading out cornmeal while I opened a can of salmon. November was winding down, and Daddy had pretty much relieved me of my cooking duty after all the disasters. Still, Grenna kept hope that I'd "catch on" over time. So she was determined to teach me how to make salmon croquettes today.

"There he is again. My little hummingbird just blurred by the window," she said in her I-have-the-best-word-for-Scrabble voice.

"Well, I don't see anything but the old maples and a few dandelions in the straggly grass of the backyard," I said in my oops-you-picked-a-word-that's-not-a-word-and-don't-you-feel-foolish voice. I'd hoped she'd given up on the hummingbird thing by now. I knew there might've been one hanging around in September or even October, but in November, no way.

"Well, keep the feeder full, because he's been coming to visit almost every day," she said before turning her attention to our cooking lesson. "First, we need to shape the salmon into patties."

I tried to mash the pink fish into a patty, but it kept falling apart.

Grenna started humming as she whipped the cornmeal and egg with a fork. It was a song from one of the old records Kevin had played for us the night before. "Hmmmm mmmm mmmm . . . when I see you again . . . after the war . . . when bluebirds sing . . ."

*Oh, no,* I thought, *there she goes again,* as she started into her story of the sweet little place where she and Grandpap lived. "We didn't have room to turn around twice, but we had the sweetest view from our windows. Remember, March Anne," she said, "a mansion's made of windows, not of walls."

Then, peering out the window, she said, "And, March Anne, never forget that the biggest dreams grow in the small-est houses."

The next thing I knew Daddy and Kevin were coming in through the front door.

Kevin tossed his soccer ball into the corner, and Daddy exclaimed, "Hoo-whee, something sure smells good in here!"

A little later, when we sat down at the table, I realized that I'd gotten lost in Grenna's story once again and didn't have the foggiest idea how to make a salmon croquette.

The day before school let out for Thanksgiving break, Laverne passed a note to me after homeroom. I unfolded it and read it while Mr. Farkle was still hopping around the science room chanting, "They shall crunch peanuts, they shall crunch toes, and they shall make science wherever they *goes* . . ."

*Dear Josephina,*

*Hi. I'm writing this to implore you for a name change at the next Pseudonymph meeting. I simply can't get into Raquela. Maybe it's because my eyeballs are about to pop out looking for nonexistent peanut mold . . .*

*Later, Reluctant Raquela*

Before English class, Meg handed me a note in the hall. I read it while Mrs. Rulanger was busy writing the quote of the day on the blackboard.

*Dear Josey,*

*I guess you've heard from Laverne, and we're fed up with the "foreign" names. Desiree sounded so beautiful at first, but it really doesn't fit me. Maybe it's because I'm spending so much time with Jim after school. We're making great progress on the Flop Effect project. By the way, it looked to me like you and Benjamin were discussing more than squash beetles at the library yesterday . . . What's the scoop?*

*Soon, Discontented Desiree*

During class, Mrs. Rulanger explained that a semi-palindrome was a word that you could read both forward and backward, like *mug* and *gum*. That set me to thinking that maybe Meg, Laverne, and I could find our winter names within the letters of our given names instead of in the yellow

144

Pseudonymph book. When I'd finished my in-class essay, I wrote notes telling them of my idea. After class, I passed the notes to them, and they read them before the next bell rang. On the bus ride home, we agreed to the new name idea, and set the official name-exchange date for the first Saturday of December.

## Seventeen

*I* woke up at dawn with determination.

The week before I'd heard Grenna ask Daddy if he could pick up a "ready-made" Thanksgiving dinner from the Piggly Wiggly deli. That would not happen in this tiny yellow farmhouse—not if I could help it.

I'd found Daddy later and told him that I was cooking the Tanner Thanksgiving Meal. This time, I resolved to myself, I was going to get it right.

Turkey. Dressing. Cranberry sauce. Green beans. I'd even planned another pumpkin pie for dessert.

Grenna hadn't felt well during the night, and she was napping the morning away. Of course, at first I was at a loss, so I looked through the recipe box again. Seeing the words written in Grenna's own hand made me think of her other words, her spoken words. The lilt of her stories was somehow there in her looping *l*'s and curving *g*'s.

I snapped myself back to the task at hand and took the turkey out of the freezer, salted and spiced it as the recipe card instructed, and put it in the oven to roast at 425 degrees. So far, so good.

By midmorning, Kevin and Daddy were watching pregame football shows. Daddy would look over at me every once in a while and ask if I needed help, but I always refused. I had to do this on my own.

As it approached noon, I crumbled the corn bread and left-over biscuits from Burma's and mixed them with salt, pepper, and sage into a casserole dish.

After lunch, I started in on the cranberry sauce. *Mash two cups of fresh cranberries.* These were the simple instructions Grenna had written on the page. As I measured out the red-purple berries, I was reminded of the red azaleas that bloomed in our yard in the spring. Azaleas always reminded me of Grenna's story of how she and Grandpap spent their honeymoon on the Yellowbell Express. I could hear her voice telling me the story.

*Your grandpap held out his hand, and I stepped right up into that* Dreamliner *like the queen of England!*

*It was the sweetest time.*

*And guess what, March Anne? We stepped off that train in Virginia, and it was spring. Spring again!*

*Sweet.* Something about the word snapped me back to the present.

Yes, the turkey smelled wonderful.

* * *

Thanksgiving dinner was a disaster, of course. After everyone was seated at the table, I pulled out the turkey for Daddy to carve. But when the knife tried to slice through the meat, it wasn't done. I hadn't realized that the turkey had to *thaw* before I roasted it. The turkey went back into the oven, hours away from being roasted thoroughly. Somehow, in all the commotion, I also forgot to add eggs to the dressing, and it was dry and too crumbly. The cranberry sauce and green beans were passable, but who could eat cranberry sauce and green beans for Thanksgiving?

Finally, Grenna roused herself and scooted Ellie into the kitchen. Daddy and Kevin looked lost in the mess. I was close to tears.

"Hmmm," Grenna said, opening the refrigerator door and surveying its contents.

"Well, I guess it's time the Tanners had a peanut-butter-and-jelly Thanksgiving," she said. "We can have our turkey feast tomorrow."

"But, Grenna," Kevin whined, "we can't eat peanut butter for Thanksgiving!"

"Holy gladiolas," Grenna chided, "why not? Your grandpap and I did on our first Thanksgiving after we were married. Peanut butter was hard to come by then. Yes, we felt ourselves in high luck to have it!"

I looked over Grenna's shoulder and peered into the fridge. "We do have some grape jelly," I said.

"Oh, then we shall have a feast indeed," Grenna cried, her eyes sparkling. "And, Bradley, get the peanut butter from the cupboard. I'll just grab this here loaf of light bread.

"Kevin," she added, a smile flickering at the corner of her mouth as she looked at our amazed faces, "you get the round-robin quilt and spread it on the living room floor and we'll meet you there in a jiffy."

We sat down with the simple fare on the quilt, and I had to admit that I was feeling a little better already.

We couldn't help giggling as we spread the peanut butter and jelly on our bread. Daddy pretended that the peanut butter had stuck to the roof of his mouth, and when Kevin made an emergency milk run to the refrigerator, Grenna and I hooted with laughter.

When we gathered in the living room later that evening, after the mess was cleaned up, I noticed that we were smiling contentedly. Our Thanksgiving dinner had been the simplest of meals, but it had proved to be most satisfying.

The next day, when I checked on Grenna, I heard her say in her sleep, "Just look there—he's come back—all dandied up with a red band at his throat and a thousand hemidemisemiquavers of light dancing on his green silken coat."

I jotted the words down in my notebook, wondering if they were part of a famous poem. Since I couldn't ask Mrs. Rulanger about it until next week, I looked up *hemidemisemiquaver* in the dictionary instead. The definition read: "A sixty-fourth note. The smallest unit of musical time. Chiefly British."

*Hemidemisemiquaver.* It was a long word. A wonderful word. I just couldn't figure out what a measure of "the smallest unit of musical time" had to do with green silken coats.

By Sunday, with squiggly-lined football games, Nancy Drew, and Sunday preaching to distract me, I'd pretty much forgotten about the unusual word.

On Monday evening, Grenna felt up for a game of Scrabble. Daddy had been out on the highway in Comet that day and started things off pretty quietly by earning 12 points for SEMI.

Grenna, however, thought the word was the best thing since peanut butter. She squealed and clapped as she built QUAVER onto Daddy's SEMI for 28 points.

"What?" Kevin barked. "That's not a word."

"Hush, melon brain," I said. "We'll look it up if we need to at the end of the game, like always." Of course, since I'd already looked up something similar three days before, I figured Grenna knew what she was doing.

Kevin consoled himself by building on Grenna's A to spell out GAG and smiled and smirked, even though the word was worth only 5 points.

Of course, when I added LOLLY to his GAG, Kevin's smile vanished and was replaced with my own.

Daddy built on Grenna's Q to spell out SQUASH, which also was a high scorer for the night. But when I spelled PAL in one turn and added the letters crossing the R in Grenna's QUAVER to spell PALINDROME on my next, I thought for certain sure I had everyone beat.

"No way, that's Japanese or something!" Kevin cried. I just smiled and shook my head. Mrs. Rulanger had taught me better.

Taking her last turn, Grenna added DEMI to her SEMIQUAVER to rack up a Tanner all-time high of 96 points for one word. Once again, Grenna reigned supreme, clapping her palms and grinning like the four-year-olds at the church nursery.

Kevin seethed and ran for the dictionary.

"Face it, Kevin," I said as he found the word. "Next to Grenna, we're nothing but a bunch of squash beetles."

Part Three

# Eighteen

*U*nder the naked white branches of Maranatha, Meg, Laverne, and I looked at one another to gather our courage before we began peeling off our coats. We were wearing bathing suits underneath our clothes, so we weren't exactly skinning down to our skivvies, but it sure felt like it in the cold air.

Laverne and Meg had spent the night, and we'd woken up at dawn to make it here for our Pseudonymph ritual. As agreed, we'd rearranged the letters in Meg, Laverne, and March to discover our newest names.

We stood on the stone-hard earth. It was hard to believe that this was the same dirt we'd turned so easily with our trowels just a few months before. Of course, there was no sign of the bulbs we'd planted back in the fall on this first Saturday in December, but a bit of the metal rail was still exposed like a cold, bare bone.

Flip-flopping around Maranatha in a Hawaiian-print one-piece, Meg started the ritual. "As the trees are free of summer leaves in winter, we now shed our clothes." When she spoke, her breath made little white puffs in the cold air.

Laverne and I adjusted our bathing suits and followed her: "To feel the winter wind, to feel the newborn cold."

Meg continued: "Now, when the earth is bare, we will reveal our new true names."

Meg stopped, turned toward Maranatha, raised her arms, and said: "No longer Meg, my name is Gem."

Laverne stepped beside Meg, raised her palms, and added: "Laverne is but an echo of my real name, Ravenel."

I tripped over a root as I filed into place and lifted my arms beside my friends before announcing: "March has no place in the coming winter. I am Charm."

We walked around the tree three more times, chanting "Gem, Ravenel, Charm." Finally, we all yelled: *"Hot chocolate!"*

We laughed at our silliness and the exhilaration of the cold as we hurriedly pulled back on our clothes.

Then, like the littlest piggies, we ran back to the farm, with Meg's flip-flops clapping for us all the way.

$\mathcal{G}$renna was on all fours peering under her bed.

"What in tarnation are you doing?" I asked.

Grenna told me she was still looking for her white flannel gown.

That did it. I needed to take immediate action.

Later that day, Daddy and I jumped into Comet and headed to town to shop for fabric. There usually weren't big crowds in Jubilee, but Main Street had cars backed up five deep at the traffic light. The toy shop and jewelry store seemed to be particularly popular. I supposed people were beginning their holiday shopping.

We finally found a parking space by the bank and walked back up to our destination, Calico Corner.

Daddy had already given Grenna a mail-order gown, but like the one from Belk's department store, it didn't keep her warm enough. Daddy told me that Mama had sewn the gown out of some extra-thick flannel for Grenna years ago.

That news had given me the idea to make a gown for Grenna for Christmas. Meg and Laverne had agreed to help me sew it during the holidays. We were too busy now. Mr. Farkle and Mrs. Rulanger were working us overtime. Our science projects were due the day before we let out for break, and Benjamin and I were furiously crunching squash beetle numbers, recording the final juice recipe, and writing up the report.

Calico Corner had a particular odor, maybe of a hot iron, and I found the smell strangely familiar. I ran my hand down a row of cotton fabrics printed with little pink checks, blue polka dots, and tiny bunches of roses.

Daddy told the saleslady what we were looking for.

She frowned. "Yes, we used to carry that kind a few years back, but I'm not sure that we have any left. I'm not even sure if they *make* flannel of that quality anymore."

We followed the lady through a maze of fabric displays to the sign marked "Flannels." There, sure enough, was a bolt of fuzzy white material, but I could tell without even touching it that it was thinner than the Belk's gown. It simply wouldn't do.

The saleslady saw how disappointed we were, so she said she would check in an old storeroom in the back. In the meantime, I went to look at patterns. Daddy helped me pick out the lace and buttons recommended for the gown.

"You'll also need some good-quality white thread for the sewing machine," Daddy said.

I looked up, surprised that he knew anything about sewing.

"Your . . ." he began, looking down. "Your mama used to love this store. That last year she was sewing all kinds of baby things for Kevin. She brought you here several times before she . . ." Daddy stopped, unable to say the word.

"Died," I finished for him. We looked at each other, the word hanging between us under the buzzing fluorescent lights.

The saleslady returned from the back room looking somewhat ruffled and not a little dusty.

"I found some," she exclaimed, holding up a bulging bag. "It's only about a quarter of a bolt, but it should be enough."

She took the material out of the bag and expertly measured the length at a yardstick. "Six yards," she said.

I grinned from ear to ear. It would be more than enough.

December 5th was the first time I saw the hummingbird Grenna had been hooting about since October. Of course, I'd probably seen him during the summer with the other hummers, but I hadn't taken the time to notice one as different from another then. Unlike Grenna, I hadn't seen a hummingbird at the globe feeder since school started.

But on that afternoon in December, I'd been sitting in Grenna's bedroom telling her about how Benjamin Hartwell had messed up our squash beetle display by shoving pink erasers in it to look like a smiley face.

Grenna was listening, and when she laughed, I noticed something green glimmer and flit outside her window.

But when I looked again: nothing.

I started telling her about Meg's new Rollerblades and how

she'd almost broken her arm already when I saw something again. A flicker.

I looked again: nothing.

When I started telling Grenna about Laverne's wish for a new puppy, I kept my eyes on the feeder, and, sure enough, in the next moment, a bright little bird hummed itself into view.

Suspended by its whirring wings, it stretched its ruby throat toward the feeder and sucked nectar through its built-in straw. The colorful bird looked like something ripped from a tropical island and glued against a brown, bare world.

I was speechless.

"Yes, isn't he beautiful?" Grenna asked. "He's been visiting me every day. I've named him Zipp."

*Well,* I thought, *at least Grenna isn't completely wonky.*

The hummingbird buzzzoommed over to the front oak. It did seem like he was zipping through the air.

"The name fits him," I said.

"Actually, I named him after Moses' wife Zipporah, in the Bible. The name means little bird," Grenna said, her eyes twinkling as green as Zipp's shiny coat of feathers. "I figured that women were named after men all the time," she said. "So why can't men be named after women?"

Mrs. Rulanger was always saying things like that at school. "My English teacher would be proud," I said, smiling back at her.

The two of us watched Zipp needle back through the bare, reaching branches and whir away.

Grenna shut her eyes and smiled, as if she was somehow following him in her mind as she rested.

I was glad to see her smile, but as I closed Grenna's bedroom door, I couldn't help thinking how different my grandmother had become from the energetic little bird who'd decided to lengthen his usual summer visit.

In science class the next day, I told Mr. Farkle about the hummingbird.

Then things started happening.

A few days later, Mr. Farkle and two science teachers from the high school came to take pictures of our little hummingbird.

Not long after, Kevin's science teacher showed up with a video camera.

On December 12th, a special bird scientist called an ornithologist came to tag Zipp. He told us that Zipp is a western species that should have migrated to Mexico for the winter.

Grenna grew concerned at this news. "Is it wrong to leave the feeder out?" she asked him.

"Oh, no," the scientist reassured her. "No amount of food will prevent a bird from responding to the changing seasons. Something else has kept that little hummer here."

After the ornithologist came, the newspaper showed up. By the time school let out for the holidays, Zipp had been on the six o'clock news, filmed for a bird documentary, and was scheduled for the February cover of a nature magazine. Birdwatchers from as far away as Milwaukee came to stare at our little winged wonder.

Grenna lay in her bed through most of the hubbub. Sometimes she would make it over to her window with her walker and watch for a while. Mostly, though, she would stay in bed and rest.

# Twenty

Laverne had planned her annual Christmas party for seven o'clock.

The invitation was open to every kid in Sunny Brooke who was around Laverne's and Michael's ages.

Naturally, Benjamin Hartwell and company lived in Sunny Brooke.

Meg and I arrived at Laverne's house at six. We'd purchased Pseudonymph charm necklaces at the Jubilee jewelry store with our Watermelon Festival popcorn money, and we were ready for our official gift exchange. This Christmas, Laverne's two new Lab puppies, one chocolate and one black, greeted us at the door. They were early presents to Laverne and her brother from her parents. The puppies dashed between our legs as we trooped up the stairs to Laverne's room.

Laverne's bed was covered with a lavender sateen comforter, and filmy purple curtains hung from the windows. We stood beside the bed as Meg pulled a tiny white box from her coat pocket and handed it to Laverne.

"A raven for Ravenel," Meg said as Laverne opened the box. Laverne slipped the silver chain around her neck and clasped it under her blond curls. Then she gazed, smiling, at the charm of a silver raven holding a tiny black onyx in its mouth.

My fingers picked at the tightly taped box that Laverne gave me. Finally, I opened the box and revealed a silver shamrock on a thin, silver chain—the name *Charm* was inscribed on the back of the clover.

"Gosh, thanks," I said, straining to clasp it beneath my thick hair.

Within the box I'd brought, Meg found a small ruby pendant.

"A gem for Gem," I said. The red stone glittered and sparkled as Meg held it up to the light. "It's beautiful," she said.

Wearing our charms, we went downstairs to help with the last-minute party arrangements. Everything was festive, with logs glowing in the fireplace, carols crooning from the stereo speakers, and lights winking and flashing on the tree and mantel. As we set out paper cups and napkins, the black puppy took a particular liking to Meg's jingle-bell-studded flip-flops. The pup had almost chewed clear through one of the straps before we were finished pouring ginger ale into the fruit punch and the doorbell rang announcing the first arrival.

Laverne's parents seemed to be fine tonight: smiling at all the right times, talking nicely to each other, and taking turns coming around with trays of cookies and pigs in a blanket. Or were they were just putting on a show for the holidays?

A carol streamed from the speakers. *Well,* I thought, listening to the words, *there are no chestnuts, but we do have lots of popcorn, chips, cookies, and pretzels.* And, though there weren't many jingle bells, the doorbell was definitely ringing.

Laverne was speaking to Colette Violetti and several other people I recognized from school. I'd seen Colette and Benjamin sitting together on the bus on the last day of school before break. Were they becoming an item? The popcorn I'd munched on turned to lead in my stomach.

Meg was in a group with Jim McClendon. I decided to join them. Jim had started talking to Rodney Carver about football, and Meg took the chance to whisper loudly to me, "Jim and I have permission to go the movies tomorrow night."

"Wow," I whispered back over the crooning Christmas carols. "Is your mom driving?"

She nodded and turned back to Jim while I headed for the punch table.

As I took a sip, I glimpsed Benjamin Hartwell standing under the mistletoe in the doorway between the kitchen and the living room.

I couldn't help but notice that he wasn't just standing there—he was looking at *me.*

I set down my punch.

I started toward him. It was almost as if I was being drawn across that warm room by those eyes of his.

Halfway across the room, I felt something tug at my ankle. My jean cuffs were being attacked by the Lab puppies. I reached down to free my legs from the squirming little dogs, and when I looked back at the mistletoe, Benjamin was gone.

I searched the room. Yes, he had definitely left the party.

A few minutes later I also noticed, with a little sinking feeling in my heart, that Colette Violetti had made herself scarce.

In theory, I thought Benjamin Hartwell was mildly disgusting.

In theory, I thought Benjamin Hartwell was *weird*.

In fact, Benjamin Hartwell might have left the party with Colette Violetti that night.

And I went home feeling blue.


"Timber!" Daddy yelled after he sawed through the last edge of cedar bark.

It was the cedar I'd admired in the fall, and I knew it would make a perfect Christmas tree for us. In a way I hated to see it felled, but Grenna had explained to me how it was important to bring something of the forest into the house at least once a year.

Yet the day wasn't quite right.

The buttons on Daddy's red-and-black-checked tree-hunting shirt were about to burst open over his pumpkin stomach the same as always. As usual, Kevin was tugging on the tree trunk like a bulldog on a bone.

But, this year, Grenna was at home in bed.

Grenna had always come with us to cut the tree. And no matter how much my head kept telling me that everything was the same, my heart knew that everything was different.

"We'd better be heading back," Daddy said as he took hold of the middle of the cedar to help Kevin tote the tree.

We started down the path under the bare winter branches of the hardwoods. The forest was a wash of gray, reaching bark.

Here and there, green still asserted itself in prickly holly leaves replete with red berries or the long needles of a pine.

*Well,* I thought, *at least Grenna will be able to help decorate the tree.*

Daddy began singing "Silent Night."

Kevin and I had just chimed in when a small object buzzzz-whirrrrred by me.

I flinched in surprise.

"What?" Kevin asked.

"I don't know," I said. "Some kind of huge bug nearly nabbed me."

Daddy twisted his neck around like Blynken in the barn. "Well, it seems to have gone now."

We started on "O Tannenbaum."

*Whirrrbuzzzzz.*

"There it is again!" I cried.

"There is *what*?" Kevin demanded. "I didn't see anything."

"I'm not sure," I admitted. "It might have been a hummingbird."

"What did it sound like?" Daddy asked.

"Kind of like a tiny motor," I said, thinking hard. "Or like a woodpecker trying to peck really fast on . . . a basketball?"

Kevin chuckled.

"All I know is I'm sure I've never heard that sound when we've chopped down our Christmas tree before," I said.

The both of them had started looking at me like I was wonky when the little green creature sawed right through the frosty air between us.

"There it is!" Kevin yelled. "It's a miniature alien helicopter, otherwise known as Grenna's hummingbird!"

"Yes, it *is* Zipp," I cried.

I'd suspected this Christmas was going to be different, but I never knew it would be *this* different. Our tree already seemed to have its first ornament: a very colorful and active ornament.

As we continued on, the hummingbird ziiiipped this way and zaaaapped back the other way.

"I think we just nabbed Zipp's home for our Christmas tree," Kevin observed. "And now we have one irate hummingbird on our hands."

"Well," Daddy said. "If it wasn't its home, the bird definitely seems possessive of this tree."

When I caught sight of the yellow gable of our farmhouse

through the trees, I broke into a run. I couldn't wait to get home and tell Grenna.

"Grenna," I cried, stumbling into her room. "We saw Zipp! He followed us home. Well, actually, I think he might have followed *his* home here."

Zipp flew to the feeder. I couldn't help noticing how he seemed to chug along his own little invisible train tracks in the air. Sometimes zooming forward. Sometimes backward. Other times stopping at a midair railroad crossing with Nandina and Shout.

"Oh my, there he is," Grenna said. "March Anne, mix some more nectar. The feeder is a little low. Use lots of sugar, now."

"Yes, ma'am," I said. I mixed the nectar, adding an extra dash of sugar. Outside, I replaced the feeder while Kevin and Daddy steadied the cedar into the tree stand inside.

Zipp made a dive *for my nose.*

"That does it!" I announced as I walked through the screen door. "The tree is going back outside. I won't be able to hang an ornament on that tree knowing it rightfully belongs to Zipp."

Kevin protested at first, then he shrugged. "All right," he said. "I guess it will be kinda cool to have Christmas outside this year."

"We can decorate the mantel and the stair banister," Daddy said, "but if we leave the tree outside, it will have to be au naturel."

We knew we would miss decorating the tree, but it was for the best. After all, Zipp would have to get used to his tree being in a new place. He didn't need to deal with tinsel and ornaments, too.

Daddy placed the tree in the yard, and we watched him water it from Grenna's picture window.

"My, my," Grenna said. "Isn't that cedar a pretty sight? It will be nice to have little Zipp living so close to home."

## Twenty-one

*H*ave you seen him?" I asked, rushing into Grenna's room after lunch the next day.

"Come," Grenna said, patting the bed. "I was just watching for him."

I sat down on the quilt, and for a while it was quiet and still. I could hear Grenna's light, measured breath. I'd decided to keep track of the little bird myself over the holidays, and we hadn't seen him all morning.

For a moment, I was afraid Zipp wouldn't come back. Maybe he'd decided to follow the bird-watcher back to Milwaukee.

But then Zipp perched on top of the red globe.

"Now that," Grenna said, "is grace."

"*What* is grace?" I asked.

"Zipp's being *here, today*," she answered. "Grace is a gift. It's always a gift of love, but it usually comes in an unexpected way."

Grenna reached over and put her wrinkled hand on mine as we continued to watch.

"Today is the first day of a new season," she said. "And, in all my days, I never dreamed I would see a hummingbird in winter."

Later in the afternoon, the Pseudonymphs convened in my room for a mission that would require our combined resources: sewing the new white flannel gown for Grenna.

"I *think* I remember how to put the thread in," Meg said, fumbling with the new spool Daddy and I had bought at Calico Corner.

We'd already dusted off the old sewing machine from the hall closet, lugged it up the stairs, and placed it under my bedroom window. Meg told us that her grandmother had tried to teach her to sew once, so we were relying heavily on her past experience.

"Unfortunately, Charm, the news is downhill after that," Meg continued. "I tried to sew an apron that weekend, but it turned out to be a . . . *blob*. Even my grandma agreed it was fit for nothing but the dump!"

With the thread in, Meg tried pushing the foot pump, and the needle started going up and down at a steady rhythm that was, again, strangely familiar to me. Just then something outside the window caught Laverne's eye.

"Is that Zipp?" she asked.

We opened the window and saw Zipp zazooming from his

perch on the bare branch of the front oak to the red feeder. I'd told them about Zipp, and they'd seen him on the news, but this was the first time they'd had the chance to meet him face-to-face.

"It sure is," I announced.

"Oh, he's *gorgeous*," Laverne said.

As we pinned pattern pieces to material and cut white flannel, Zipp kept twinkling by our window to say hello. He even perched for a moment on my windowsill.

"I think Zipp is in love with the sewing machine," Meg said, pushing the pedal and starting it back up.

When the machine quieted down and I was trying to determine if the stitches were straight, Laverne said, "Speaking of being in love, Gem, tell us about your big date with Jim McClendon."

Meg looked up—a little red in the cheeks. "I am *not* in love," she protested, grinning from ear to ear. "Well," she admitted. "Not very much, anyway."

We burst out laughing.

As I attempted the next seam, Meg told us about the movie and how much she had enjoyed the project for Mr. Farkle's class that we'd finished just before the break.

"His toes showed a separation of five millimeters in three months—isn't that amazing?" she asked. "I mean, we actually proved a scientific hypothesis."

"Yes, I can see it now," Laverne teased. "Meg Fincher and her assistant Jim McClendon receive the Nobel Prize in science for successfully proving the Flop Effect."

Meg laughed good-naturedly at the joke, but I was grimacing. My seam definitely wasn't straight.

"Oh no, guys," I groaned. "It looks like I might be as good at sewing as I am at cooking!"

As I carefully picked out the crooked seam, Meg pulled a pendant out of her blouse. It was a heart; on one side was inscribed "Meg" and on the other side "Jim."

"This *is* serious!" I exclaimed.

Meg shrugged, but she was still beaming.

"What about the squash beetles, Charm?" Meg asked.

"Overall, the project was a success," I said. "We concocted the world's best beetle juice. So, next fall, beetles beware. Benjamin is even thinking of bottling the repellent and selling it at the Watermelon Festival."

"Oh, I found out why Benjamin left the party early," Meg told us. "He had a basketball tournament the next day, so his parents came to pick him up. Colette had to duck out, too, because of her ballet recital."

"Well, my project was a real flop in every sense of the word," Laverne said, returning to the science subject. "Rodney and I had peanuts in the shell and peanuts out of the shell. We had peanuts inside the house and peanuts outside the house. And guess what? Not a one of them even thought about molding—zilcho, nada—not even a trace of mildew. So we had to write it up in our Farkle report as 'a work meriting further study.' Speaking of tragedies," she added, "I've lost the Pseudonymph raven charm that y'all gave me."

"Already?" Meg asked, taking over at the sewing machine again. "You've only had it a couple of days."

Laverne explained how she was wearing it when she was playing with the puppies in the front yard, but the jabbering crows in the pine tree finally chased them in. At supper, she'd looked down and noticed that it was gone, chain and all.

"I jumped up from the table and ran outside, and just before dark, I found the chain," she said, pulling the thin silver chain from her pocket. "But, even though I've looked till my glasses froze to my nose, I couldn't find it anywhere. The raven charm is *gone*."

"We'll come over and help you look for it," I offered. Then I ventured to ask her, "By the way, Rave, how are things in the parent department?"

"Not so great. I can tell they're trying because it's the holidays . . . but they seem . . . tense. I almost wish they'd start squawking again like the crows, the silence makes me nervous."

It had grown dark and our backs were aching when Laverne finally repaired my disastrous seam.

"I'll go down and make us some popcorn," I announced. I could tell this Pseudonymph venture was going to be an all-nighter.

And I'd discovered that sewing could leave a body famished.

At about 4:30 a.m., Meg finished sewing on the last of the lace trim.

Then she crawled into bed. Before long I heard a light whiffling snore to match the even breathing of Laverne, who'd zonked out at 2:45.

I threaded the needle one last time. The only things left were the buttons, and buttons I could do.

The next morning was Saturday, and we crawled out of bed when Daddy called us. Meg's mom was picking both Meg and Laverne up at eight o'clock. It was only two days until Christmas. Meg was heading to the mountains with her mom, and Laverne's family was leaving to visit her grandparents in Tennessee. Daddy was starting out early himself to meet with someone at a bank in Atlanta—something about making ends meet on the farm.

Meg, Laverne, and I admired the white flannel gown hanging from the top of my closet door one more time; then we folded it and put it in the robe box I'd found in the hall closet. We wanted to go ahead and give it to Grenna while we were together.

After a short breakfast of cornflakes, we knocked on Grenna's door.

"Come in," she said.

She was sitting propped up on her pillows, but I could tell that she was just waking up because her white hair was a little ruffled, and there was no trace of pink lotion in the eucalyptus rub air.

"Merry Christmas," Meg said, placing the box on her quilted lap.

Laverne walked over to the other side of her bed.

Grenna gazed at the box and reached out and held Laverne's hand and Meg's hand, looking at them each in turn with her bright green eyes.

"What a surprise, girls," she said. "I wasn't expecting such sunshine in December!"

Grenna opened the box and gasped with delight.

"My nightgown," she murmured, stroking the soft, fleecy material. "It's even more beautiful than I remembered."

I could tell that Grenna's words were thick with emotion, and I thought I spied a little tear trickling down her left cheek when we heard the *beep, beep* of Meg's mom's hatchback.

"Oh, Grenna," said Laverne. "We've got to go."

They each gave Grenna one more squeeze of the hand and quietly said, "Love you," before they started for the door.

"I love *you*, girls," Grenna called after them.

Grenna struggled to the edge of her bed. She grabbed Ellie and made her way over to her mirror.

"March Anne," she said, "help me put this on."

I'd never helped her dress before, and I realized it must be getting harder for her. When we slipped off her thin gown, I was shocked by how tiny Grenna was.

The new gown went easily over her head, and she began buttoning it in the front.

"I'd forgotten about these sweet little buttons," she said, smiling at herself in the mirror. "Where was the gown hiding all this time?"

"Actually, Meg, Laverne, and I sewed—"

Grenna was already talking again. "It's as soft as a cloud. They don't make flannel like this anymore."

"That's true, the lady at Calico Corner told Daddy and me—"

Grenna interrupted again. "Just look at this lace, it's pretty enough for a wedding gown."

"Grenna, what I'm trying to tell you is . . ." I began to say, but my grandmother turned her head this way and that, smiling like she was a model in a magazine. I heard her say softly, "Yes, it is pretty, Anne, isn't it? It's the prettiest gown I ever saw."

I realized then that Grenna wasn't really in her bedroom with me. She was in another place and time, with the white flannel gown that her daughter had made for her.

As I slowly started up the creakity stairs, I heard her call after me, "March Anne, were you saying something?"

"Oh, no, Grenna," I called down to her. "It's nothing."

For when I'd seen the morning sun picking out the bright gold in Grenna's green eyes, I'd suddenly known that gown wasn't about me or Laverne or Meg and our all-night sewing marathon. It wasn't even about thick flannel. The real warmth of the gown was caught up in a memory of something long ago. And it was for certain sure that the best gift I could give to Grenna that morning was to keep my mouth shut.

# Twenty-two

*T*he news broke later that day. The forecasters were predicting snow and a deep freeze for Christmas Eve.

Normally, I would have been ecstatic for a white Christmas, but not this year. I ran to Grenna's room.

"Grenna, it's supposed to snow tomorrow night! What'll we do?" I asked her, frantic. The weather report had said the temperatures would drop to freezing after sunset. "Should we bring the feeder in? Should we try to bring Zipp inside, too?"

Grenna was quiet for a moment. Finally she said, "Zipp chose to stay the winter with us, and we'll just have to hope and pray he'll survive it.

"You know, March Anne," Grenna continued, adjusting the quilt over her legs, "I'm kind of like Zipp. Most of the people I've known and loved in my life have migrated on to a better place. Your grandpap, my sisters, my parents, your mama. Sometimes I don't feel I'm fit for this world of televisions and fast cars, just like I'm sure Zipp feels out of place in this bare, cold season."

I looked out the window for a minute at Zipp's thin red scarf. His green feathers were beautiful, but much too flimsy to keep him warm.

"Still, I'm glad he's here with us," I said.

"I am, too, child," said Grenna smiling at me. "I am, too."

I knew we needed to act fast.

Unfortunately, Daddy had gone to Atlanta in Comet, and we didn't know what time he'd be back.

At two o'clock, Kevin and I decided to call the ornithologist who had visited us for advice. We had to leave a message.

We kept waiting by the phone, and, at four o'clock, he called us back. He told us to have at least two feeders and a hair dryer. We would have to keep vigil during the night, and when one feeder froze up, we would have to replace it with the thawed feeder. We could use the hair dryer to thaw out the one that was frozen. He also said that, depending on the temperature, the nectar could freeze every hour or so.

We had only the one feeder. Trouble was the stores would be closing in Jubilee at five, and the next day was Sunday, so they wouldn't open at all. I had to make it to town in less than an hour to buy another feeder.

I decided to call the Feed 'n' Seed before I left.

Benjamin Hartwell answered the phone.

"Hello, Benjamin, this is March Anne Tanner. Do you have a hummingbird feeder in stock?"

"A hummingbird feeder? For Christmas?" Benjamin asked in surprise.

I reminded him about our small green visitor.

"Oh, yeah," he said. "I'll go back in the storeroom and see what I can dig up. I'm pretty sure I've seen some feeders in our summer stock."

"Thanks," I said. "By the way, could you wait if I'm a few minutes late? I appear to be . . . Well, let's just say I'm *transportationally challenged* at the moment."

I couldn't quite bring myself to admit to Benjamin that I was actually planning to ride Spunky all the way into town.

Kevin helped me saddle up the old mule. He decided to stay home and keep tabs on Zipp and the temperature. I looked at the horizon. I simply had to make it to town and back before dark.


"Looky, Mommy, it's Santy on a reindeer!"

"That's not a reindeer," the woman said as I made my way down Main Street on Spunky. "It's a mule."

*Please, Lord, don't let anyone recognize me.* I tried to pull my face deeper into my hood, wondering what had possessed me to choose a *red* winter coat this year. To wear a red coat with the hood up at Christmas was a little much. To wear a red coat with the hood up at Christmas while riding a mule down Main Street was *over the top*. But the temperature was dropping, and the wind was burning my cheeks. I couldn't afford to be vain, given the circumstances.

Along the way to town, cars had slowed down and children had waved and pointed. I'd waved back, reminding myself of my noble mission.

Main Street suddenly felt endless.

As I passed Town Hall, I glanced up at the clock. It was nearly 5:15. It'd taken me longer than I'd expected. I hoped Benjamin was as good as his word. I'd have hated to be making this humiliating ride for nothing.

Downtown Jubilee at Christmastime was always a beautiful sight. Burma's Biscuit Barn kept festive lights blinking and winking in the windows even after they closed. Elegant white lights studded the lush swags of green garland under the awning of the antiques store.

The Red Caboose toy shop came into view, with its brightly lit window displaying teddy bears and dolls and wooden soldiers. The clerk was just flipping the door sign to "Closed" as people filed out with bags of toys, and I had a warm flash of remembering the Christmas wishes I'd made at that window over the years.

As Spunky was clip-clopping her way past the jewelry store, several girls spilled out the door; they were closing up, too. I recognized Colette Violetti's hair at once. Was that a fur coat she was wearing?

I ducked my head, but it was too late. I'd been spotted.

The girls pointed, and I could hear them giggling.

*Please, Lord, don't let Spunky decide to take a dump at this moment.* I faced the wind and pushed toward my goal.

Finally, I tied up Spunky to a tree at the First Federal Bank, hoping Benjamin wouldn't actually see how I'd been transported to town. I should've saved myself the trouble, because when I looked up, Benjamin Hartwell was already making his way across the street. He must've been on the lookout from the store porch.

"I'm sorry I'm late," I said, glancing back at Spunky and blushing warmth into my already red-from-the-cold cheeks.

"You rode that old gal all the way here?" he asked in what sounded like an admiring tone.

"Yeah, like I said, Daddy's gone to Atlanta, and I had to get the feeder today to help our hummingbird survive the freeze tomorrow night."

"Oh, yeah, it was a madhouse in the store today," he said. "I didn't realize how many people buy presents for their animals!"

He shoved a bag toward me.

I grabbed it and looked inside at the feeder. "Great," I said. "How much do I owe you?"

"We had to close up shop on time—everybody wanted to get home, you know, with the weather and the holiday. So, just consider this a present from the Feed 'n' Seed."

"Are you sure?" I asked.

He nodded and walked back over to Spunky with me.

"Hey, you think that old gal could stand double duty?" he asked. "I kind of missed my ride home."

The sun was hovering just below the gathering clouds.

"Sure," I said, patting Spunky on the nose. I was anxious to get home, but I knew that, even traveling a bit slower, we'd make it before sundown.

I climbed into the saddle, and Benjamin clambered up behind me.

Let's just say that the ride home was not as humiliating as the ride to town. Somehow, when you're riding a mule with a guy with melted-chocolate eyes sitting behind you, it's not so bad—even if you are still wearing a red coat.

I asked Benjamin about his search for the hawk's nest, and he said that he'd had to slow down the search for the winter, but since he'd staked out the territory last fall, he was hoping to sight one in the spring.

As the sign for Sunny Brooke Acres subdivision came into view, the first flurries fell onto our faces. I pulled off my hood.

"You can let me off here. I know you need to get back and all." Benjamin nodded toward the bag.

"Okay," I said, noticing that it was almost dark. As he was pulling himself over to dismount from the saddle, I felt something almost as light as the snow but decidedly warmer brush against my cheek.

"Merry Christmas!" Benjamin called once he was down from the saddle.

"Merry Christmas," I called back, feeling quite toasty despite the fact that the flurries were thickening.

On Christmas Eve, Grenna dozed most of the day as the snow continued to fall off and on. At sundown, the fields on the Tanner Watermelon Farm were blanketed in white and the temperature had plummeted well below freezing.

By that time, Kevin and I also had the hummingbird survivor plan in action. We were simply changing feeders every thirty minutes, before the nectar had a chance to freeze in the spouts. When we brought a feeder in, we placed it by the fire in the living room to thaw. I wished I could let the hair dryer blow warm air over Zipp, but I was afraid the noise might spook him, and I knew he wouldn't last long away from the food—his only source of warmth—during the snowstorm.

Kevin was on duty for the moment. He was playing some of the old records in the living room, and I could hear the lyrics wafting up to my room as I took a break.

I plugged in the single white electric candle in my bedroom window, thinking about how much I would miss the Christmas Eve service at Mars Hill Baptist Church this year. Of course, the service and everything else in Jubilee was canceled because of the weather.

Still, I would miss the candlelit sanctuary, and I would miss seeing the carolers under the streetlamp on the corner of Main Street. But, for now, it was nice to remember yesterday's ride on Spunky, and to sit by my candle and look out at the newly white world, and to say a prayer for a certain green bird.

About 3:00 a.m. the snow lightened to flurries, although the air was still freezing. Daddy came in carrying more firewood. "Zipp's still zipping," he said.

I noticed Daddy seemed to be glad to have a mission this

Christmas Eve. His face was unpinched for the first time in weeks. Instead, his cheeks were glowing bright red from the brisk cold.

We looked at Kevin, who, much to his later chagrin, had already fallen asleep on the couch. I snapped off the record player.

Daddy put a quilt over Kevin. Then he turned to me. "It's about time for you to turn in, too, little girl."

"Little?" I said, looking down at where my ankles were poking out from the bottom cuffs of my jeans.

He laughed. "Well, little or no, you'd better get in bed. You don't want to scare Santy Claus away. Don't worry, I've had enough coffee to keep me awake till noon next Tuesday. I'll keep changing the feeders."

"Okay, Daddy," I said, looking at the clock, "but I need to do one more thing first."

That was really a fib, for I actually intended to do several more things.

First, I checked in on Grenna, who was sleeping peacefully in her soft flannel gown.

Then I checked on Zipp through the window. We'd left the outside light on, and I could see him fussing at the cold and sipping away at the feeder. The snow, now, had definitely stopped.

Next, I refilled my mug of hot chocolate and sat in the living room for a few more minutes by the fire. Kevin was still snoozing under his quilt. Daddy was sipping his coffee and watching the squiggly lines on the TV with the volume turned down.

And then, only when I had finished my last sip of cocoa, did I step back out into the cold night.

I always liked to visit the barn on Christmas Eve. Grenna had brought Kevin and me out here every year when we were younger, telling us the story of how Jesus was born in a stable. I was most fascinated by the legend of how animals could talk on Christmas Eve. And, although I wasn't really expecting to have a conversation with Spunky, I was always hopeful when I entered the barn on the holy night.

My boot soles made a whispering crunch in the blanket of white snow, and when I reached the barn door, I kicked my boots to free them from the white fluff. Inside, the smell of hay was not nearly so strong as usual in the still, freezing air.

I flicked on the lantern, and, as my eyes adjusted, I could see that I wasn't too late. Wynken, Blynken, and Nod were still on their roost, their huge eyes shining. The owls were awake.

Spunky stuck her head out of her stall to see what the commotion was about. I walked over and portioned out a small helping of oats.

"Merry Christmas, ol' girl," I said, letting the mule eat out of my mittened hand. I tousled her mane and plopped down onto a particularly inviting pile of straw near the door.

It wasn't long before Dorcas emerged from the shadows of

the hayloft. She hopped down the ladder and nestled in my lap, warm and purring.

Just when my nose felt like an ice cube and my toes started to numb and I was beginning to think I was wasting my time, I heard the whisper of wings. It was more of an awareness of motion, really, than a sound. Then I caught sight of them— Wynken, Blynken, and Nod—their wings spread impossibly wide and white inside the barn. With one accord, they bowed their noble heads, glided through the loft door, and lifted off into the night.

I jumped up and ran out with them. This was what I'd been waiting for. And I was amply rewarded.

The wind had pushed the banks of clouds into the distance, and a band of stars now glittered in a deep river of blue overhead. The owls flew out across the fields, seemingly ignorant of both the newly whitened world below them and the sparkling jewels above. The next moment, though, I realized that it wasn't ignorance, really, but a deeply held wisdom. For they held in their very feathers an intimacy with snow and sky.

When the threesome reached the far fringe of trees, I expected the owls to lower into the branches for their nightly hunt. Instead, the massive white birds soared higher. And I lingered there in the cold, watching them continue to journey onward and upward. Pondering how, on this most holy of nights, we shared the seeking of a star.

# Twenty-three

When I awoke the next morning, sunlight was filling my room. I looked through my frosty windowpane. The Tanner Watermelon Farm was still covered in a deep blanket of snow. A white Christmas! We'd had snow in Jubilee before, but never in time for Christmas.

Bounding down the stairs, I was greeted with the smell of frying bacon. I peeked through the living room to see Daddy busy in the kitchen cooking Christmas breakfast. He smiled and raised a spatula in my direction. My tummy was growling, but I couldn't think about food.

I ran through the open door to Grenna's room. Kevin was already there.

"Grenna," I cried. "It snowed! What about Zipp?"

But Grenna wasn't in her bed. In fact, she wasn't in her room at all.

"Where is she?" I asked.

"Out there," Kevin said, pointing at the window.

Outside, Grenna was bundled up in a pink chenille robe, a green woolen hat, a bright red scarf, and even an ancient purple shawl for good measure. Her skinny metal elephant of a walker stood beside her in the snow.

"Well, come on!" I yelled to Kevin.

We tumbled and stumbled over each other by the front door, pulling our coats and boots on over our pajamas. Finally, we ran through the screen door and out into the cold morning.

"What are *you* doing out here?" I yelled to Grenna. Each word made a puffy cloud in the frigid air.

"You didn't think I was going to miss my first white Christmas, did you?" Grenna asked, her eyes bright with laughter. "Zipp and I have been waiting our whole lives for this."

"There he is!" Kevin yelled.

We looked up to where Zipp was perched on the snow-covered cedar tree.

He had survived. He had survived the freezing night.

We stood there in the quiet of the morning, staring at the strangely miraculous sight of a red-scarfed bird so tiny and impossibly green in the middle of a newly whitened world.

The sun rose a little higher in the sky. And suddenly a million hemidemisemiquavers of light and color sprang to life in the snow.

Taking this as his cue, Zipp zigged through the blue and violet twinkles at the top of the tree and tapped his skinny beak at a little ice droplet. Then he zagged back by orange and red shimmers to a lower branch and sampled a snowflake. Up and down, back and forth, swerving and hovering, Zipp circled the tree as if he were stringing glittering tinsel. The sight was absolutely magical.

"That's what a Christmas tree is *supposed* to look like," Grenna declared.

"Merry Christmas, Zipp!" Kevin hollered, throwing a handful of snow into the air.

Zipp buzzed to his feeder.

I watched him perch on the red globe and begin to sip at the nectar.

"Now that's grace," I said.

"What's grace?" Kevin asked.

*Grenna,* I thought.

*Christmas,* I thought.

*This hemidemisemiquavering world,* I thought.

But I only smiled and said, "A hummingbird in winter."


Christmas was the usual rush of morning excitement and then the lull time when we didn't really do anything but watch football games or old movies or read or nap or look back over our gifts until mealtime. This Christmas, even the lull was punctuated with a few more small triumphs before the day was over.

We knew that money was tight, so Kevin and I were very glad for the new pairs of Levi's and sneakers left by Santa Claus.

Grenna gave me a journal that had a leather cover tied with a simple string. I didn't know what I would write in it, but I liked the feel of the leather in my hand, and I liked how the paper was scented with the faintest whiff of eucalyptus rub.

I gave Grenna a snail I'd made with round stones I'd gathered from the creek in the woods. I had glued the stones in a spiral for the shell, using a long curving rock for the body, two tiny pebbles for eyes, and twigs for antennae.

Grenna looked at it and smiled. I offered to put it on her windowsill with her other tackies.

"No," she said. "I want to keep it here with me for a while."

I watched as she felt the smooth stones with her fingertips, a faraway look in her eyes.

Kevin gave us each a tie-dyed T-shirt. He'd somehow managed to create a design that looked just like the green squiggly stripes of Rattlesnake watermelons. Grenna laughed and slipped hers over her white flannel nightgown, and we agreed to wear them for Christmas dinner.

Later, I set the table with an old poinsettia tablecloth from the hall closet, our pair of crystal candlesticks, and candles that were as bright as Shout's red feathers. I also placed out our best dishes and green cloth napkins.

*I might not be able to cook, but even I can handle setting the table,* I told myself.

Daddy lit the candles, Grenna added a red silk neckerchief to her watermelon T-shirt, and everything looked festive and bright and lovely. The red and green reminded me of little Zipp, and I was glad that he was warm and fed as well. The temperatures had climbed all day, melting most of the snow, and the feeder was brimming full. Now I had my own Christmas dinner on my mind. After spending the night feeding a hummingbird, I'd worked up quite an appetite.

The triumph of the evening was the food. Not *my* triumph, mind you, but Kevin's. I was more than glad to let him have the glory of it. Oven-roasted turkey, mashed potatoes and gravy, green bean casserole, and even biscuits.

Grenna took a few bites. "With a little more shortenin' and a little less knead, Santa Claus will be stopping by next year for biscuits to set his reindeer flying," she said.

Kevin beamed.

But Daddy and I had no critiques. All we could do was nod and eat. This was no small compliment from a girl who'd seen the cook wipe his nose on his palm at least nine million times.

After our feast, we sat in the living room by the fire and talked about playing Scrabble, but we were too lazy to get the board out.

When Daddy stood up to stoke the fire, I got up, too. I knew that the temperature was well above freezing, but I wanted to check on Zipp anyway. There was no sign of him. Probably snoozing away in the cedar, I thought.

Kevin was playing some of Grandpap's old records in the corner.

"Zipp appears to be catching some badly needed z's," I announced when I returned.

"Good," Grenna said. "Good."

"Well," Daddy said. "Zipp seems to be getting all the attention around here, since I see two very neglected socks up on the mantel."

*Socks?*

*Mantel?*

Kevin and I looked at each other and yelled, "The stockings!"

We'd completely forgotten about the stockings!

Part Four

# Twenty-four

On New Year's Day, Meg, Laverne, and I trudged across the frozen fallow field to the far fringe of trees. Meg, for once, had taken off her flip-flops and slipped on my old barn boots. She'd decided that, for her "foot health," she should exercise other shoe options at times to counteract the Flop Effect.

We were each carrying a plastic leaf bag to sit on when we reached our destination. The afternoon was overcast, just tending to drizzly, but not very cold. It felt good to be outside and for the bustle of Christmas to be over.

"How was the visit at your dad's, Gem?" I asked. I knew she had headed to Atlanta for a few days after she and her mom got back from the mountains.

"Great!" Meg replied. "We went to a hockey game and to the art museum. He even took me to see the *Nutcracker* at the Fox Theatre."

"Cool," I said. "How was your mom? I mean, without you there?"

"Fine, as usual," she said. "But I think she wants to start dating a guy at her work."

Farther on in the dim woods, three crows cawed and fussed at our invasion before lifting themselves away on their jagged black wings.

"I'm sick of crows!" Laverne said. "The puppies are so spooked they won't even go into the front yard to do their business anymore."

Meg and I both knew the crows weren't the only thing bothering Laverne, but we just nodded.

"Furthermore, I *still* haven't found the raven charm," Laverne added.

I reached up and felt the shamrock charm hanging from the silver chain at my neck. I'd forgotten to wear the charm more days than not, and the truth be told, it didn't seem to be bringing me much good luck. I didn't say anything to Meg or Laverne, but, somehow, I didn't feel like Charm today.

We arrived at the sweeping white trunk of the bare-armed Maranatha. We sat down on our huge plastic bags and gazed silently at her graceful, sculpted elegance for a moment. The comforting smell of old leaves settled into our noses, and somewhere deep in the woods a mockingbird started to sing.

It was time to make our New Year's wishes—the Pseudonymph version of resolutions.

"Okay, I guess it's my cue," Laverne said, standing up and adjusting her glasses. She loudly cleared her throat and began to speak. "The new year begins with a moment. In that moment, everything changes. The old is swept away, forgotten, and we are free to begin again."

Meg and I stood up and fell in behind Laverne.

"As I, Ravenel, step into this new beginning, I wish . . ." Laverne's voice thickened on the "wish" part, and I knew she was wishing that her parents would get their act together and remember how to be happy. But all that must've been too hard to say, because when she finally found her voice again, she said only "I wish them crows would get out of town."

Laverne fell into line behind me as Meg took the lead. "As I, Gem, step into this new beginning, I wish . . ." I figured that Meg's real wish probably had something to do with Jim Mc-Clendon, but she finished out with only "that my toes will one day return to normal."

It was my turn. "As I, Charm, step into this new beginning, I wish . . ." I felt my voice trip over the word *wish* when I realized what I really wanted to say:

*I wish that Daddy wasn't so worried all the time.*

*I wish that Grenna wasn't sick.*

*I wish . . . I wish that my mama hadn't died.*

But every time I tried to say any of those things, a lump as big as North Carolina lodged in my throat. I noticed that we'd made our way to the uncovered rail, so I blurted out, "I wish them bulbs would come up pretty."

Then the three of us walked home through the drizzly day as quiet as Wynken, Blynken, and Nod at noon. And, this time, we didn't even have the slapping claps of Meg's flip-flops to break the silence.

* * *

We arrived at Laverne's house at 4:00 p.m.

I was staked out behind the rail of the front porch.

Meg was peeking out the door of the garage.

Laverne was crouching behind a Camellia bush.

Kevin, dressed out in camouflage, was waiting behind a boxwood shrub.

Today was the day that we were "taking care" of the crows. Laverne had put up with them long enough. Kevin was always eager for a chance to put his slingshot to use.

It took about forty-five minutes, but finally we heard the rough-edged barking of the crows in the distance. A few moments later they came into view, their bodies cutting ragged, black triangles into the blue of the sky.

When they'd both landed in their nest, Kevin took the first shot. The crows cussed loudly at him, but they weren't concerned enough to leave.

With the fifth try, Kevin hit one with a rock. It started flapping and flying and squawking up a storm. The other crow also started making a ruckus in the nest and then stopped to glare at us with one eye. But when Kevin raised his slingshot again, the crow scratched at its own nest, as if tearing it up, then shook the straw off its feet, lifted off into the sky, and followed its mate toward the Point.

Kevin stood up behind the boxwood and smiled like he'd done something to be proud of—and, this time, he had. Laverne was just shaking his hand in thanks when a breeze suddenly gusted through the yard. That's when we saw the straw and leaves of the crow's nest come floating down and scattering across the yard.

*Wait a minute,* I thought. *Was there something shiny in that last dump?*

I poked the straw clump with a stick.

"What are you doing?" Laverne asked. "That stuff is disgusting."

I didn't say anything in reply because, in the next moment, I saw it: small, silver, and gleaming in the sun, it was the raven charm.

I'd remembered Grenna telling me that crows sometimes collected odd bits of glitter in their nests, but I'd never suspected that they'd rooked Laverne's Pseudonymph gift.

"How gross!" Laverne exclaimed, picking up the charm. "I've got to sanitize it."

Meg, Kevin, and I laughed as we watched Laverne run into the house, calling for her mother.

The next day was back to school. After I climbed off the bus, I strolled slowly up the driveway thinking about my upcoming Farkle test and wondering if I had time for a short snooze with Dorcas in the hayloft. It was a warm January afternoon, a day stolen from April, and something in me yearned to stretch into the sun-warmed hay for a while.

That's when I saw Grenna sprawled out on the ground beside the barn.

Her skinny elephant had taken a tumble, too, and was leaning into the nandina bushes.

The breath seemed to squeeze out of me as I ran to her.

"Grenna! *Grenna!* Are you all right?"

She smiled at me weakly. "Well, yes and no," she said. "Just help me up."

I pulled her up, and she shook her head as if to clear it before she began pushing her way back toward the house.

"Grenna, what in the world were you doing out here?"

"I was bringing some food out behind the barn for an old friend," Grenna said, choosing her words carefully. "I haven't been able to get out much this past year, but I was lying there in my bed this morning thinking about our leftovers in the fridge. I couldn't help but think how she must be so hungry, you know, with no one to look after her."

*O Lord,* I prayed as we entered the house, *please don't let her start with the wonky talk.*

"I was scooting around the side of the barn when Ellie slipped right under me, and *boom,* down I went with her," Grenna continued.

As I helped Grenna into bed, I couldn't help but notice that her hair was mussed up and that her face looked as white as her gown. I got her some water and saw a note saying that Daddy had gone to visit Mr. Mack to discuss starting a beehive in the middle of the watermelon patch.

It was only when I tried for the third time, unsuccessfully, to punch Mr. Mack's phone number on the telephone that I realized I was trembling.

\* \* \*

Later that day, a doctor came to check on Grenna. She hadn't broken anything, but they wanted her to go to Atlanta for tests. Daddy took her the next morning. They would be staying overnight.

Whenever we weren't at school, Kevin and I rattled around the house with Mrs. Gertrude Mason like three dried-up seeds in a hollowed-out gourd.

When he and Grenna got back from Atlanta, two days later, Daddy sat Kevin and me down at the kitchen table and told us the doctors had found that the damage to Grenna's heart had worsened and there was nothing they could do. "It's just a matter of time," he said.

I didn't like the sound of that.

It sounded too much like a matter of *fact*.

# Twenty-five

A few days later, I brought Grenna a tray of fruit after school, and we sat and watched Zipp at the feeder for a while.

She was in bed and sleeping almost all the time, and nurses were coming in regularly, but, for now, her eyes were bright and glinting green.

While we ate, I told her about the strange thing that was happening in Mr. Farkle's science class. I'd dubbed the phenomenon "Weird Science."

I was still paired with Benjamin Hartwell. After explaining about the two almost-kisses Benjamin and I had shared, I told Grenna about how every time I opened my mouth to say something to him, the word *weird* popped out.

"Take this past week, for example," I said. "Mr. Farkle handed out the microscopes and slides and started hopping around the room chanting, 'Bacteria, Bacteria, Wherefore art thou, O Bacteria?' Benjamin picked up two petri dishes and held them up like Mickey Mouse ears over his head and said, 'Anybody seen Donald?' "

Grenna hooted.

"I *meant* to laugh, too," I said. "Instead, I shook my head and said, 'Weird.' "

"Later, as we looked at a slide of a paramecium, he said, 'Hey, I heard we're having spaghetti for lunch. Anybody want some paramecium cheese?' "

Grenna giggled.

"I *meant* to laugh again, too, and say, 'That's a pretty good one,' but I rolled my eyes and said, 'Weird.' "

Grenna snorted.

"But that's not the end of it," I continued. "After viewing the amoeba, Benjamin said, 'Quick, what did the amoeba say to the other amoeba?' to which I shook my head. Then he quipped, 'Have you hugged your dinner today?' "

Grenna chortled.

"Grenna, I promise that I meant to say, 'Enough with the jokes, already,' when I blurted out—you guessed it—'Weird!' What's wrong with me, Grenna?"

Grenna was laughing so hard that she had tears running down her cheeks and the tray on her lap began to tilt wildly. "Nothing's wrong with you, child," she said between spurts of mirth. "You're just being *twelve* years old."

I really was concerned that Benjamin thought I had a speech dysfunction or a severely limited vocabulary.

Still, I couldn't help myself. When Grenna continued to

hoot at my perplexed look and the grapes fell off the tray and started bouncing across the floor, I joined in and hooted, too.

Strangely enough, being let off cooking duty didn't come as a relief.

I needed something to do.

Something to occupy me so that I could forget the nurses who were always noiselessly gliding between the kitchen or the bathroom and Grenna's bed. Something to take my mind off the doctor who came and went. Came and went. Almost every day. In silence.

I devoted myself to my schoolwork. I designed a budget for my personal finance class. I wrote two complete sonnets, diagrammed all my eighteen sentences early, and revised a paper for Mrs. Rulanger.

All the while, I noticed that Kevin was spending more time in the kitchen.

Tinking and tonking.

Stirring this.

Basting that.

Though most nights we were eating the frozen dinners that Daddy was now buying by the dozen at Piggly Wiggly, every once in a while Kevin would repeat his Christmas miracle and present us with a perfectly roasted chicken. Or a batch of seasoned green beans. Or a dish of broccoli with cheese sauce.

And I had to admit that he was becoming less pesty with every minute he spent in the kitchen.

* * *

When I woke up the next morning, I realized it was Sunday. But I wasn't sure if we were going to preaching.

Daddy had come into my room the night before and told me that the doctor said, "Any day now."

I'd cried myself to sleep. Then I woke up in the night to nothing but the glare of a too-silent half-moon and cried myself to sleep again.

Now I crawled out of bed, walked quietly down the stairs, and peeked into Grenna's room. Right when the eucalyptus and pink lotion scents reached my nose good, she opened her eyes and looked at me.

"Look," Grenna said, pulling back her quilt for me to snuggle in beside her and gazing out the window. "Zipp's here for breakfast."

I cuddled beside her, but I didn't want to look.

"I can't take this, Grenna. I can't take *this*."

"I know, child. It's the hardest thing to say goodbye, but we all must do it."

"I don't know how."

"Oh, fiddlehead ferns, March Anne. None of us know how. It's just something we've got to endure. We never get to know. We simply get to choose."

"Choose? Choose what?"

"Choose life, of course," Grenna said, as if it were the clearest thing in the world. "That's what the Good Book tells us, and near the beginning, too. The Lord says, 'Choose life.' It doesn't mean bad things won't happen, it just means that there's enough good mixed up with the bad to make life worth living. March Anne, no matter how bad things get, don't go taking all the good for granite."

Even though Grenna looked weak, and she was talking more slowly than normal, her eyes were bright and clear.

I was stubborn, though. I wasn't ready to choose anything. I was sad and mad and confused.

I stared out the window where Zipp was perched on the feeder, letting the winter sunlight fall right smack-dab on his ruby throat.

Grenna finally asked, "Do you know Mrs. Crutcher? She lives down in the woods near Willow Bank Creek?"

"Crabapple Crutcher? The old lady who drowns cats and poisons dogs and French-fries blackbirds with lightning rods?"

"Yes," Grenna said, flatly. "Though I don't know that I believe *all* those tales. Some of that is pure nonsense, but there's a truth in it, too. She's a hard woman now because she never got over losing her ma and pa and then losing their land. She shut out her friends and let her heart grow black and bitter."

Grenna was quiet for a minute, and I looked out beyond the hummingbird feeder to where Nandina and Shout were taking their morning sunbaths in the bare arms of the front oak.

"Mrs. Crutcher is who I was leaving the food for the other day when I fell," she continued. "You see, through the years she's come sometimes to get leftover food from the farm: tomatoes, watermelons, pumpkins, and such. That's the old way in the country—to help out those who can't help themselves. We don't ever talk about it, mind you. We just do little things like leave out food and turn our heads when something's gone missing from the garden. I guess I should have said something to your daddy about Mrs. Crutcher, but I'd always taken care of it, and he's got so much on his mind, so I didn't."

I stared out the window at Nandina and Shout, realizing finally how Daddy's watermelons had gone missing and, of course, about the witch with the pumpkin on the edge of the field at Halloween. I'd suspected it was Crabapple, but I didn't really understand why until now.

Grenna's green eyes followed my gaze, and then she added, "Everything that grows changes, March Anne. Some grow good, some grow bad. Only we can choose which way."

"But it hurts, Grenna," I said. "Why can't I just *choose* to make the hurt go away?"

"I don't know. But you can decide what to do with the hurt. You've got to search out the good in it. I don't know how, but it's there somewhere. Your job right now is to keep a lookout for your next glimpse of good."

*Glimpse of good.* For some reason that phrase reminded me of the rail that Meg had discovered back in the fall within the roots of Maranatha. I told Grenna about it.

"Oh, yes, that's right," she said. "An old timber railroad used to run right through this land in my papa's time. How do you think these fields were cleared? They cut this farmland and sold the timber down in Atlanta."

"Where does the rail lead to?" I asked.

Grenna was quiet for a minute. Then she said, "I don't rightly remember the way. Perhaps one day you should follow it and find out."

"I don't know how since I'm never going to get up from this bed," I told her flatly.

"Well, if you don't, then you'll fare no better than Crabapple Crutcher," Grenna said, touching her silver cloud of hair and studying Zipp at the feeder. "If you don't get up and go on, March Anne, your heart will be good for nothing but a blackbird roost."

On Thursday after school, I dodged a nurse and checked on Grenna. She was talking in her sleep again.

*The rails lead to the sweetest little place nestled in the dappled shade.*

*Oh, hello, Samuel.*

*Yes, I see you there all dandied up in your Sunday suit.*

*Hold the train, I'm coming.*

*I'm almost ready to go . . .*

I jotted it down in my notebook.

After a while, Grenna woke up and looked up at me with weak, dreamy eyes.

"Did you know that you say poetry in your sleep?" I asked, grinning despite myself.

"Oh, don't pull an old lady's leg, March Anne Tanner," she said, her tired eyes brightening ever so slightly.

I looked at the stationery where I'd jotted what she'd murmured and read the words.

"Well, don't that beat all!" she said between soft little gurgles of mirth. "You'll have to put me on the evening news. I've become the world's first sleeping poet."

Then she laughed.

And I laughed with her. Even though part of me felt like crying.

Every day for the next two weeks, I checked on Grenna when I got home from school.

Usually I would find Zipp flitting and flickering back and forth at the feeder. Sipping from one little plastic cup and then sampling from another. Busy, as always.

And, usually, I would find Grenna asleep. Sound asleep.

Sometimes I would refill the feeders or dust off her tackies on the windowsill. Other times I would just sit and watch her chest rising up and sinking down.

It helped me know that she was still breathing.

That she was still alive.

*Up* . . .

. . . *and down.*

But her breath was growing weaker and weaker.

She looked so calm, so peaceful. Sometimes she even seemed to be smiling.

*Up* . . .

. . . *and down.*

But she was slipping further and further away.

Some days I turned the news on extra loud so she could hear. Other times I turned up Grandpap's old records on the record player.

*Up . . .*

*. . . and down.*

But she stayed quiet through it all.

I kept denying it.

*Up . . .*

*. . . and down.*

But there were to be no more good days with Grenna.

I didn't see it then, but I can imagine now how it happened.

How Grenna opened her eyes and trained them on Zipp feasting away at the feeder on that chilly February morning.

How the sunlight twinkled in the red globe and glanced and glittered on Zipp's feathers.

How that glimmer of green was the most beautiful thing in the world to Grenna.

Then she laid her head back on her pillow, and with all that red and green still trapped behind her lids, she realized she was ready to go.

When she opened her eyes again, Zipp was waiting for her. And the wonderful thing was that neither windowpanes nor walls concerned Grenna now. She flitted right out to him, pretty as you please.

Everyone was going about their morning as usual. And, although green had become a precious thing in February, everyone was too busy to notice the shimmering glitter of *two* hummingbirds as they made their way across the bare brown tangle of the Tanner Watermelon Farm.

Not caring if they were noticed or not, the tiny birds continued on, not toward the far fringe of trees, or toward the small town óf Jubilee, but soaring up, making a beeline for the white clouds sailing across the cold blue wash of winter air.

What I did see that day was my daddy.

I had just walked in from school, and he was sitting at the kitchen table. He was hunched over a little. His overalls weren't buckled right, and his eyes were heavy with sadness.

I knew when I saw him.

Even before he said a thing.

"Come here, March Anne."

I walked over and stood beside him because he looked like he needed someone to hold on to.

And then he said the impossible words.

"Grenna's gone."

After that, all I remember is black. Everything went numb.

I knew that there was something I desperately needed to do. I also knew that I had to wait.

Then I was standing at the family plot in the pine thicket.

I was vaguely aware that the preacher was saying something. That a squirrel was scampering in a branch above us.

That Kevin was crying. That Daddy was there in his dark suit. Yet the only thing I could do was stare at the patches of sky beyond the pine needles.

That blue sky was a mystery to me, and I felt that, if I could just look at it long enough, I'd figure out all the answers to the questions of life.

Like why things are given, only to be taken away.

Like why I was picked out to become an expert on *gone*.

I felt like I was disintegrating into a million pieces, but every time I began to float away, sadness grounded me like gravity.

And so I stood there looking at the sky. I just didn't understand how it could be so beautiful when I was in so much pain.

I looked and looked, but I never could get any closer to figuring out the mystery. 'Cause that blue kept screaming back to me the only thing I knew for certain sure.

I was twelve years old.

And I was saying goodbye to the last of my mothers.

That night I slept like a rock at the bottom of a stream. Solid and dark and still.

When I woke up, the winter sun was straining weakly through my bedroom window. I could hear clinks and clanks coming from the kitchen, and I knew that Kevin was up and cooking. Everyone deals with grief differently, and this was his way.

I was glad he was cooking because I was hungry. Ravenously hungry. And to do what I needed to do, I needed to eat. Ever since that moment at the kitchen table with Daddy, all I could think about was that day when I had crawled in bed beside Grenna. That was the day we'd talked about Crabapple Crutcher. It was also the day I'd told Grenna about my glimpse of good: the train tracks in the forest. When Grenna died, I knew I had to get back to those tracks.

I dressed warmly: long johns, turtleneck, wool sweater, jeans, wool socks. I stuffed an extra set of clothes, including mittens and a stocking cap, into a knapsack. I also wrote out a note explaining where I was going and why. At least as best as I could say. I still wasn't exactly sure myself, except that it was caught up in the calls I'd been hearing since last summer and in Grenna's passing away.

The smell of frying bacon seeped under the crack of my closed door and awakened my hunger once again.

I stuffed the last of my necessities in my knapsack and headed down the stairs.

Kevin had already served up my plate of bacon and fried eggs and set it on the kitchen table. I sat down and started to eat. He went back to the stove, scooped some grits into a bowl, and set that beside me, too. I noticed him silently observing my clothes, my bag, and the note I'd laid on the table. I was glad when he picked up the note and read it by the stove. I wasn't up to explanations. The note would have to suffice for him and for Daddy.

Kevin seemed pleased that someone was there to appreciate

his cooking. While I ate the warm, buttered grits, he started gathering things in the kitchen. He wrapped what appeared to be a large chunk of ham in aluminum foil. He filled a thermos with hot chocolate. He also grabbed a plastic bag and put various things in it: half a dozen chocolate chip cookies out of the jar, a chunk of cheese, three huge apples, six freshly made biscuits, a large bag of boiled peanuts, three bottles of water, and a box of waterproof matches.

After I ate, I pulled on my coat and boots by the door and grabbed my knapsack. Kevin shoved the bag of food toward me. I nodded my thanks. I guess I should have hugged him. But I couldn't. Not yet. Right then the only thing I could do was *go*.

After I gathered a trowel and work gloves from the barn, I set out across the barren, iron-hard field. The far fringe of trees looked stark and brittle against the milky sky.

Before I entered the woods, I heard the crunch of gravel. I looked back and spotted Comet easing up the drive. Daddy slowed the truck when he saw me. I turned and continued on my way. In a moment, I heard the crunch of gravel again.

Now Daddy knew I was going somewhere on my own.

I hoped the note would be enough for him to understand why.

## Twenty-six

When I reached Maranatha, short, spiky blades of green were poking up from the ground. They were the tips of the bulbs I'd planted with Meg and Laverne. I looked at the green spikes not really to see them but as markers for the place for me to kneel on the earth and begin to dig.

I clawed at that earth with the trowel. I was secretly glad the earth was hard and cold, because I wanted to work for every inch of rail. I wanted to use every muscle of my body to dig out the rail until I was pure motion.

*Motion. Task. Digging.*

I dug through the hard layer of earth with the trowel in my right hand. Scraped it back. Raked it back. I pulled out roots and dug with my left hand until my fingers began to ache and my wrist started to tingle.

In large stretches, the rail was beneath only a shallow layer of sand. But in other spots I'd find deeper red clay, or a brown layer where the warmth seeps up from some bubbling lava center far, far below. The layer warm enough for moles and voles and chipmunks to blanket through the winter. I scraped that away, too, until I heard my trowel clink upon the hard, steel rail.

At one point I took off my gloves and dug with my bare hands. I let the soil pack tightly under my fingernails. Let my hands grow red and rough and numb with cold.

All the while I was clearing off the railroad. A rail laid by the sweat of men long ago. Sweat now gone. Reborn in me. Men now bones buried like this metal trail.

I brushed away the soil, let the rail shine in the light of day once again. Something to follow. A monument to movement. Yet there was no one left to travel upon it now except me.

And I didn't know where I was going.

The first time I stopped to rest, I collapsed on the ground. I looked back and I couldn't see my beginning point. I'd made steady progress. I was vaguely aware of the sun traveling across the sky above me, but I was completely free from clocks and calendars.

When I reached the cedar thicket, I sensed a greater stillness, an even more intense solitude. I lingered here because I wanted the outside of me to match how I felt on the inside.

Alone.

Then the tears came. I was digging under the weak yellow sun when I first felt the tears hot on my cheeks and salty on my tongue. It amazed me that so much warmth was somewhere deep inside my body. Warming my blood. Warming my tears before they emerged into the air of winter and onto the cold of my skin.

*A mansion's made of windows, not of walls,* I heard Grenna say in my mind. At first I wanted to push the words back. They sharpened the edge of my pain and quickened my tears.

I liked digging into the night. Digging into the quiet of the stars, with the lazy white eye of the moon casting blue shadows across the earth. Sometimes I would hear the rustle of a fox or the sudden *whoosh* of an owl in flight. But I wasn't scared. Fear was nothing to me now, for I was nothing but motion.

*Digging. Motion. Task.*

One time I looked up and a deer was standing, watching me. Struck dumb, I held myself still. After a while, the deer loped off to its nighttime work of finding food.

I returned to my own toil. Scraping back the skin of earth. Clawing through the clammy flesh of clay.

*Task. Motion. Digging.*

The thought occurred to me that perhaps I was not just following a trail laid by unknown hands long ago. Perhaps I was also trying to create a wound in the earth big enough to hold my pain.

In places, I polished the steel spine to a high gloss. This trail leading somewhere. Nowhere. My own hands were now blistered, my nose numb and running. A permanent ache had set up in my right shoulder, and a little shooting pain coiled and uncoiled inside my bent left knee.

When I stopped to rest at dawn, I was aware that someone was watching me. And this time it wasn't a deer.

I turned to look.

"It's me, March Anne," Daddy said. "I'm here."

At first I wanted to yell, "Go away."

Or to run away myself.

He'd probably been out here watching me the whole night.

Daddy was here.

I was here.

Instead of running or screaming, I let him sit down beside me and hold me.

"March Anne, I did it all wrong when your mama died. You were so little. I thought it might be better to just . . . forget . . ."

He held me tighter.

Then he cried.

And I cried with him.

Once we were all cried out, Daddy kneeled down beside me and started digging with his bare hands. Before long, Kevin had showed up, too.

I wanted to tell them that I needed to be alone longer. Or that this was something I had to do myself.

But I knew what Daddy had said was right.

He was here.

I was here.

Kevin was here.

We needed to get it right this time.

So when Kevin kneeled at the rail and started digging, too, I looked over at him and smiled.

After digging through the morning, we stopped to eat.

It was nice to share a meal eaten with our bare hands under the bereft branches of the forest. We ate in silence, and then we started digging again.

We dug as the sun set and another night fell in the forest. I was glad now that Daddy and Kevin were with me. Somehow I knew they needed to do this as much as I did.

## Twenty-seven

*B*ecause we'd been digging up a railroad all this time, you'd think it was the most natural thing in the world for me to open my eyes the next morning and see the sleek sleeper car of a train.

But it wasn't natural in the least. For a few moments I just stood there, gaping. Unsure whether to shout hallelujah or to fall on my face in prayer. I was aware that my clothes were damp and that it had rained lightly during the night. I looked over and saw Kevin sleeping, but Daddy was nowhere in sight.

My first thought was that this metal monstrosity in the woods should be as tacky as an old Coke can on a mountain trail. But it wasn't tacky—it was beautiful. The most beautiful thing I'd ever seen. Stretching its silver presence out by the fern-lined, rock-bedded stream. Hiding like a secret jewel beneath the gray trees of winter.

Around its middle, I could still make out the faded letters:
DREAMLINER

Here it was.

The *Dreamliner*.

Finally, I walked over and pushed the narrow door, hinged in the middle, and it bent like a V, creating enough space to reveal two little stairs. I stepped up into the train car, unsure of what I would find.

At first, I could only make out the windows. From the outside I'd not noticed how large they were, but they covered most of the walls, and I could see the reaching trees outside, the first rays of sunlight glancing on the stream.

So, this was it, I thought to myself, as my eyes adjusted to the shadows. This was the sweet little place where Grenna and Grandpap had lived. I sat down at a booth built under one of the large picture windows. It reminded me of Mole End in *The Wind in the Willows*.

Kevin climbed in. His eyes were wide, saying everything that needed to be said. I followed his gaze to the small table that held a salt and pepper shaker, an ancient bottle of ketchup, and some intricately folded cloth napkins. There was a tiny kitchen, looking neat as the Little Red Hen's despite the thick layers of dust and cobwebs.

I opened one of the cabinets and found stacks of plates and bowls. Kevin opened another to find a collection of mismatched coffee mugs. In the next cabinet, there were several rusted cans of beans, a splotchy-labeled can of pears, and an invaded bag of rice. Underneath the counter, we discovered a speckled aluminum kettle, a large boiling pot, and a frying pan. I couldn't help smiling.

Before long, Kevin and I made like Ratty and Moly and set to work.

Kevin cleaned out the belly of the stove. I filled the pot with water from the stream and clunked it on the black cast-iron eye of the stove.

While I dusted the table and washed the dishes, Daddy showed up with some kindling and firewood.

In a few minutes, Daddy had a nice fire going in the little stove. We toasted some bread and fried up the ham. I made a mental note to be eternally thankful for the common sense of my younger brother as I sat down and let the warmth start to sink into me. It was the first warmth, besides my tears, that I'd felt in days. After we'd finished our food and sat sipping our hot chocolate, Kevin was the first to break the silence.

"Did you know about this place, Daddy?"

"Yes, a little," he said. Daddy's eyes searched the network of branches outside the picture window. "Your mama had told me about it. But she'd also told me about how Grandpap took to drinking here at times, so I steered clear of it. Besides, I was so busy taking over the farm that I never had time. Your mama started getting sick with the cancer about the same time she found out she was pregnant with you, Kevin . . ." Daddy's voice trailed off. He was quiet for a minute, looking thoughtful.

"One day, I couldn't find your mama anywhere. March Anne, you were only a little thing then and running wild. I was near my wit's end. Grenna and Grandpap took you to Jubilee, and I set out for the woods. Kinda like I did the other day when I came to look for you," he said, turning his eyes on me. "I knew she would be out here somewhere, just like you were.

"I didn't have any rails to follow back then," he continued, looking at the fire, "but I found her anyway. She was curled up on that mattress over there and crying. I held her for a while." Daddy hesitated and then looked at Kevin. "And that's when she told me she wasn't going to have no radiation or chemotherapy. She was going to have a precious baby. She loved you more even then, Kevin, than she did her own life."

Daddy's eyes had filled with tears again. He held out his arms to Kevin. After a minute, I mashed into the hug, too.

By the time our tears started to dry, the *Dreamliner* was warm enough for me to peel off my wool sweater and open two windows—the only two that still worked.

Then, instead of digging, the three of us set to work against at least a decade's worth of dust.

As the sun rose higher and light filled the train car, I started to notice things I hadn't seen at first. Like a small brass box sitting on the counter. I opened it up and found a pack of playing cards. A little later, I discovered a cross-stitched sampler hanging on the wall that read, "To Record the Marriage of Morwenna Rebecca McGuirty to Samuel Jones March—on the third day of May—in the year of our Lord nineteen hundred and forty-six."

The fifth time I went to dump the filthy water and get a refill from the stream, I caught a glimpse of bright and tawny red within the reaching gray of trees. It was Nandina and Shout, here for an afternoon splash and sip of water.

"You little red rascals," I scolded them. "You two knew about this place all along, didn't you?"

At the foot of the bed, I discovered an old metal footlocker with latches. It was closed securely enough to keep out critters, but I remained on my guard as far as spiders were concerned. Kevin kneeled beside me and Daddy sat in a chair, looking on, as I raised the lid.

On top were several whiskey bottles of various shapes and sizes. Some opened and half full. Some completely empty. We took them outside and opened each one and poured out the putrid whiskey—watching the brown liquid disappear into the earth. I could hear Grenna's voice again:

*Liquor'll sour the sweetest of places, and that poison did its devil's work on mine. My mansion became good for nothing but Grandpap in one of his black moods. But I can't blame him too much. He always wanted to be a railroad man, and we got waylaid here in this watermelon patch. Praise mercy his dark days were few and far in between. All in all, life was good to us. He would tell you that for certain sure if he were here today.*

Then I went back in and pulled out an old army uniform. The letters on the rectangular patch over the pocket read "M A R C H."

"Your grandpap was a soldier—in World War Two," Daddy said as we looked at the uniform. "He'd never talk about it much, but I think he went through something terrible."

Looking into that trunk, I wondered now for the first time

where Grandpap was stationed during his service. I remembered learning about the horrors of the war in my history class. I wondered how he survived with any dreams left to dream.

"M A R C H." *A soldier's name. Grandpap's name. My name.*

Among some old newspapers, Kevin discovered a stray envelope. On the front of the envelope the name Morwenna was written in blue ink.

Seeing the handwriting scrawled across that paper helped me to glimpse something in my grandpap I'd never seen in the quiet old man whittling in the rocking chair in my memory. It was strange how something written in my grandfather's own hand brought his presence before me as nothing ever had before.

The letter was written for Grenna, and the back flap was sealed tight. Had the moisture of years resealed it? Or had the letter somehow slipped between the cracks of time and place and gone unread? Lost? Forgotten?

Kevin looked at me, and I nodded for him to open it. We knew we were the only ones left for it to belong to.

*June 1944*

*Dear Hummingbird,*

*I can't wait to get back to you. Away from the dirt and grime and blood. Far away from the smell and stench of war.*

*When I get back to you, we'll build ourselves a king-*
*dom. A place to forget the sight and smell of death.*
*Will you be my queen forever? In our kingdom? I'll*
*ride upon the dream that you will answer yes.*

*Love, your Sam*


So, Grandpap had called Grenna "Hummingbird."

Kevin carefully passed the note to Daddy, and I realized that
I hadn't seen Zipp since before the day of Grenna's passing.

Later, Daddy got down on the floor, and he and Kevin continued rifling through the trunk, looking at other old letters
and medals and badges.

I found a small wooden box on top of a writing desk. Inside was a leather journal, not unlike the one Grenna had
given me for Christmas. Scrawled across the first page were
the words "Private—what is written on these pages is meant
only for the eyes of Anne McGuirty March."

I hugged it to my chest for a moment and then put it in my
knapsack. I knew that the journal, as much as the *Dreamliner*,
was what I'd been looking for all along.

When Kevin and Daddy latched the lid of the trunk, I saw
that Kevin had also collected some things he wanted to keep.

We were finally ready to leave.


Back at the house, I took a long, hot shower, and the only
thing on my mind was my bed. On my quilt were notes from
my friends. I snuggled down under the covers to read them before I fell into a deep, sound sleep.

*February 8*

*Dear Charm,*

*I saw you at the funeral, but you looked right
through me, like you didn't see me. I know this is so
hard for you. Remember I'm here. I wish I knew what
to say,*

*Gem*


*February 9*

*Dear Charm,*

*When are you coming back to school? Don't worry,
I'll collect all the Farkle and Rulanger assignments for
you.*

*This is so sad. I know that Grenna was really a mom
to you. I loved her, too.*

*Hug, Ravenel*


*February 10*

*Dear March Anne,*

*I've called you fifty times, but nobody answers.*

*I guess you're doing what you need to, but if you're
not back by Monday, I'm coming after you—Laverne,
too.*

*We love you, Meg*

*February 10*

*Dear March Anne,*

*We came here today and found the note you left for Kevin and your dad.*

*Do what you have to, but we want to be there for you. We're sad, too.*

*And we miss you.*

*Love, Laverne*

It was hard when the yellow bus showed itself on the distant hill on my first day back to school. I was a different girl from the one who'd ridden this bus just the week before. I wanted to scream at everyone I saw: *Grenna's gone. Don't you see? Everything's changed.*

But Nandina and Shout kept chasing each other through the frosty morning without her.

The daffodil blades kept slicing through the frozen ground by the barn.

And the yellow school bus was still coming down the hill.

When the bus door screeched open, I noticed that it was hinged in the middle and that it fell into a little V just like the door on the *Dreamliner*.

I knew that, as hard as it was, I had to step up and keep going to school and studying. After all, Benjamin would be relying on me for our new science topic, I had a math study date with Meg and Laverne on Thursday, and I had a paper due for Mrs. Rulanger the next Monday.

Right then I couldn't really feel the importance of that

school stuff, but I knew deep inside that those assignments were somehow wrapped up in my future. Reading Mama's journal had taught me that she was expecting me to make the most of my dreams. So, just as Grenna had always predicted, big dreams were awakening in the tiny yellow house on the Tanner Watermelon Farm.

# Twenty-eight

*I* waited to open the envelope I'd found tucked into my mother's journal.

My name was written across the front. In blue ink.

This time there was no doubt.

It was written by her.

To me.

Each morning I shoved the letter into my pocket.

Before I went to sleep every night, I put the letter in the Good Book on my bedside table. Right smack-dab in the middle with the picture of Mama. In Psalms.

On Friday, I asked Meg and Laverne to come over.

I led them down the train track to the *Dreamliner*.

I knew they needed to see it and the letter, too, or they would never understand me.

I also knew that, without them, I would never understand it all myself.

We sat on the bed in the old train car.

I opened the sealed flap of the envelope and read until my tears blurred the words.

Then Laverne read until she couldn't speak.

Meg finished the letter.

Then we held on to each other.

And I realized that friends could fill up some of the spaces *goodbye* leaves.

If they are good friends, like mine are.

If you let them.

*February 24*

*March Anne,*

*I'm writing this because I don't know how much time I have, and I wanted you to know that you are my sweet hummingbird. I always say that you learned to sing before you ever said your first word. You began last summer, right after you turned one, by humming with your grandpap's harmonica.*

*And the first time you said "Ma-ma," I swear it came out in the notes of G and E.*

*I also call you that because, like me—and hummingbirds—you are always flitting away, outside, beyond my reach and sight to the watermelon patch or to the far meadow. One day you toddled all the way to the woods and liked to scared me to death.*

*When I finally found you, I just held you and held you. Your daddy laughed at how I wouldn't put you down for the rest of the day, even when you wriggled and cried. I held you through the night, watching the moonshine catch in the little curls of your eyelashes.*

*I'm leaving this letter here. In this special place. I'm hoping for a miracle, but, just in case, I'll know it's here waiting for you.*

*I can imagine you now . . . on a cold winter day like today, flitting into the woods, seeing the wonder of this place gleaming in the sun, letting the door fall away, and stepping inside to find the words that I've left to you—with love,*

*Mama*

The next day I set out for the pine thicket with my knapsack. The afternoon was overcast and chilly, but not as cold as it had been during the dig to the *Dreamliner*. From the road, it still startled me to see the new white gravestone in the family plot.

Under the pines, I read the names engraved on the three stone markers: ANNE McGUIRTY MARCH TANNER. SAMUEL JONES MARCH. MORWENNA McGUIRTY MARCH. It might've been a trick of sunlight shifting through pine needles, but when I read Mama's name for the second time, I glimpsed a glimmer, a flit, a flicker of something I'd never seen before in that old rock.

I walked around to the back of Grenna's grave and sat down. Leaning up against the cold slab of marble, I pulled the leather journal Grenna had given me out of the knapsack. I didn't really know how to begin, but Mrs. Rulanger said that it's good to write when your heart's full, so I grabbed my pen and decided to give it a try.

*Dear Mama,*

*It doesn't make sense to write to nobody, so I decided to write to you. Let me tell you about Grenna's funeral—I can talk about it now. The sky was blue and sunshiny, the kind of bright day that Grenna liked best, and Daddy had bushels of roses spread out all over the pine thicket. The preacher prayed and read from Psalms, and a lady from church sang the hymns Grenna loved to hum. I think she would have been pleased . . .*

When I closed the journal, I felt exhausted, but I did feel a bit lighter, after all.

# Twenty-nine

**O**n the first day of March, I heard the trill of a mockingbird float from the front oak and into my bedroom window.

I called Meg. She told me that she'd started wearing slides, which were open sandals with a broad strap instead of the toehold. They still made a little slapping sound when she walked, she said. "They're softer than the flip-flops, but just as steady. The slides allow me to counteract the Flop Effect *and* let my feet breathe. I don't see how you can stand it with your feet cooped up in those sweaty sneakers. Feet need to *breathe*!"

It felt good to hear her voice as I looked out my window.

"Also, March Anne," Meg said. "My mom . . . is . . . well, she's dating."

I held the phone tighter, wondering what to say. Knowing that Meg was going to be needing Laverne and me to help her adjust to this.

I called Laverne. She told me that Jim McClendon and Meg were getting so lovely-dovey it was making her gag. Then she told me that her parents were signing up for marriage counseling. Laverne would be needing Meg and me, too.

Just like I needed them.

A couple of weeks later, I bustled into Mr. Farkle's science class right before the bell rang. It was still hard to go to school most days. But I had to go on, no matter how impossible life seemed without Grenna.

Daddy was already making preparations for planting, and he and Comet were working overtime in the fields. The green rattletrap of a truck had, that very week, conked out twice on the way to Piggly Wiggly. Kevin and I would also be working overtime on the farm soon.

As I made my way to my desk, Mr. Farkle said on cue, "We opened the door and *influenza*!"

In a more businesslike tone, he continued, "Now, everyone get with your lab partners. I want to commend everyone again on your fabulous fall projects. Peanuts, toes, and pumpkins also thank you. Several of the reports are worthy of advancing on to the county science fair. In the meantime, the winds are changing, and it's time to start another project. Begin by formulating new hypotheses today. Next week we'll discuss our plans for research. Remember that you have only one month to engage in your actual experimentation and research and two weeks to write it into a formal report."

When he finished with the instructions, Mr. Farkle started hopping around and chanting in his most patriotic tone: "Give me labs, give me experiments, or give me tests!"

"I found one," Benjamin said.

I thought he meant a hypothesis for our new project, so I looked up quickly from my notebook.

Benjamin held out a feather. It was dark brown and black with a tawny red tip. I knew without asking that it was a hawk's feather. A tail feather.

"I found it last Thursday. It's not the same as finding the nest, but it's part of the Cherokee ritual when the hawk gives you a feather."

"Wei——" I almost said *weird* for the nine millionth time before I stopped myself.

I finally found my voice again. "I mean . . . wow."

"Wow?" Benjamin asked, his dark brown eyes sparkling.

I reached out and took the feather from his hand. For the first time, I felt the elegance of its hollowed-out quill and noticed the beauty of the little painted lines that filled out the feather.

"Yeah," I said, smiling and looking back at him. *"Wow."*

On Saturday, I unscrewed the lid to the globe feeder and poured fresh nectar from the plastic jug.

I could still hear Grenna's words in my head: *four parts water to one part sugar.* I hadn't seen Zipp since before Grenna died, but I figured I'd best keep it filled, just in case.

The wartime melodies from Grandpap's records crooned

out of the open windows of the *Dreamliner* and into the cool morning. Daddy had hired a big tow truck to pull the train car out of the woods and park it behind the barn.

Kevin ran an extension cord out there and had pretty much taken up residence. Dorcas, too, had ditched the hayloft for the *Dreamliner*. Even Spunky seemed to like snorting at Kevin through the windows when the records were playing. One of Kevin's soccer buddies was coming over later to listen with him.

After hanging the feeder on the wire, I picked up my blanket of loot from the porch. I'd spent the morning raiding Grenna's dresser drawers and had found glue, scissors, old seed catalogs, medicine bottles, pink-lotion jars, eucalyptus rub tubs, and she-lack. I took the loot to the front yard and started to sort everything for when Meg and Laverne arrived. The Watermelon Festival was still many months away, but we'd decided to go ahead and start getting ready for a decoupage booth.

I spotted Nandina and Shout watching me from the still-leafless branches of the front oak, and though it was warm, the pale yellow sun seemed very far away from Jubilee, Georgia.

I cut a picture of some gladiolas out of an old seed catalog and then looked out to the front field, where Daddy was turning earth, getting the soil ready. In a few weeks, Kevin and I would be out there with him, planting seeds.

Even though it was mid-March, everything was as ugly as mud. The clover fields weren't blooming yet, and the rest of the melon fields and the yard were scraped to a dull gray-brown. Without the dignity of cold, even the bare trees looked awkward and forlorn against the milky sky.

The music continued to spill out of the *Dreamliner*, and I hummed along in little snatches as I snipped the star shape of a fiddlehead fern out of the catalog. Then I glanced up at the train car again and over to where Daddy was working in the field. Each of us was missing Grenna fiercely, but we were trying to stay busy like we knew she'd want us to. It was hard, but we were biding our time, waiting and watching. For Grenna had taught us that one day a little green hummingbird would wing its way back to the Tanner Watermelon Farm.

Grenna had taught us that one day, it would be spring again.

# Epilogue

**W**e reached Maranatha just as the sunlight was slanting across the forest floor. This was the time of day when the youngest trees—called the understory of the forest—got their direct dose of sun.

The rail I'd uncovered over a month ago was gleaming like a long snake trailing off into the distant woods, but that's not what caught our eyes. What stopped us short was a shaft of sunlight hitting smack-dab on bright purple, pink, and yellow.

The bulbs we'd planted in the fall had finally bloomed.

A wood thrush sang out deep in the forest, reminding us of what we'd come for.

As the last of the light drained away, Laverne pulled the yellow book of names and the little white box out of her knapsack. While I flicked on the lantern, she slipped the charm back on its silver chain and clasped it under her curls.

It was time to begin the spring Pseudonymph ritual, but none of us moved or spoke. Maybe it was because we had a lot on our minds that we didn't have the words for. I knew that I, for one, had something to tell them, but I didn't know how to start.

Finally, I spoke into the gray shadows. "Listen, I've been thinking, and, well, the thing is, I've come to terms with some of my name issues. It all started when we were talking about what we might name our *future* children the other day. Ravenel, I remember that you picked Madison and Jenna, and Gem, you liked Hampton and Breanna. Well, I couldn't think of anything then, but late one night, when I woke up to nothing but the sound of the first few crickets warming up, the names popped into my head: Tanner for a boy, Tannery for a girl."

I tried to meet their eyes to see how they were taking the news before I took a deep breath and continued. "Now, as you both know, those are *family* names, so there I was breaking the first and foremost Pseudonymph rule, just like that. I don't know if it's a genetic thing or not, but I was planning to do what I'd pledged I'd never do—load my *future* children up with family names."

"It's okay," Meg said.

"Yeah, I've also—" Laverne agreed, but I started talking again. I knew I was being rude, but I also knew I had to finish my confession.

"That's not everything . . ." I stammered. "I've decided *not* to change my name. It's got to do with this past year and things I've learned about March, and the fact it was Grandpap's last name, and did you know that there was a queen named Anne?"

This time I was afraid to look up, but I plunged ahead while I still had the nerve. "Well, anyway, thanks for being there for me and my name issues. I'll always be here for y'all, but I'm going to give up my membership in the Pseudo-nymphs."

We were quiet for a minute. I wondered if Meg and Laverne were staring at the ground, too, and noticing how the smell of the forest floor was even stronger in the gathering darkness.

Then I heard something that sounded like hiccups but at a quicker tempo. I realized the noise was coming from Laverne, who was bobbing up and down, her curls bouncing in rhythm with the bobs as her glasses slipped down the bridge of her nose.

"What?" I asked, smiling already.

Meg snorted, and Laverne let her giggles flow full force, and soon we were laughing so hard that we almost wet our pants.

It turned out that, ever since the crow experience, Laverne had detested her new Pseudonymph name.

As for Meg, well, she'd found that one "Jim" was enough for her.

I fished in my hair for the clasp of my silver chain. Seeing what I was doing, Laverne and Meg unclasped their necklaces, too.

After putting our charms in the little white box, we placed the box and the official copy of *Thirty Thousand Names from All Over the World* deep inside the hollow of Maranatha.

And then we walked home, with our own names, together.

# Acknowledgments

I thank God that Janine O'Malley fell in love with this story of a girl, a grandmother, and a glittering bird. Janine, my sincere gratitude for your vision and guidance in helping me tell "the whole watermelon."

I would also like to acknowledge the University of South Carolina graduate program in composition and rhetoric—namely Dr. Christy Friend as well as Dr. Mary Styslinger and the Midlands Writing Project. Dr. Dianne Johnson-Feelings—thanks for believing in my manuscripts—your support gave me the courage to proceed.

I am deeply grateful for those who believed first and longest in my dreams—my family, friends, and neighbors. Every prayer, gift of time, act of kindness, encouraging word, and happy thought you've given me are part of this book.

As a hummingbird's feathers mirror the splendor of the sun, my hope is that my words sparkle with my love for the Maker of words and worlds. To God be the glory.